It's a
MATTER
of TRUST

It's a MATTER of TRUST

Marcia Byalick

Browndeer Press
Harcourt Brace & Company
San Diego   New York   London

Browndeer Press is a registered trademark of Harcourt Brace & Company.

Library of Congress Cataloging-in-Publication Data
Byalick, Marcia, 1947–
    It's a matter of trust/by Marcia Byalick.
        p.   cm.
    "Browndeer Press"
    Summary: A teenager's life is changed forever when her father is indicted on criminal charges.
    ISBN 0-15-276660-X
    ISBN 0-15-200240-5 (pbk.)
    [1. Fathers and daughters—Fiction.   2. Political corruption—Fiction.]   I. Title.
    PZ7.B9835It   1995
    [Fic]—dc20   94-49733

The text was set in Fairfield Medium.
Designed by Lydia D'moch
First edition
A B C D E
A B C D E (pbk.)
Printed in the United States of America
Reprinted by arrangement with Harcourt Brace & Company.
10   9   8   7   6   5   4   3   2

For Bob, my best friend, my partner,
and father extraordinaire . . .
for always

CHAPTER 1

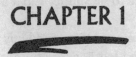

"WHAT'S THE BEST personalized license plate you ever saw?" I asked my parents, mainly to break up the monotony of the two-hour trip from our house in Nassau County to our cottage on the bay in Edgemont. We had been making the same ride at least ten times a year for most of my sixteen years, and whenever we got to the halfway point, I started to get nudgy.

"I don't know about the best one, but the most obnoxious one has to be on Jill's brother's new convertible. It says U WISH," said Allison, my best friend, who was sitting next to me in the backseat helping me polish off the box of chocolate chip cookies, the bag of Fritos, and the half pound of gum balls that we had expected would last us the entire three-day stay. We didn't always eat like that. Both of us weighed the highest number for our height on the chart in the nurse's office, so we were pretty careful most of the time. But this was the beginning of Christmas vacation, and long rides through deserted farmland were boring.

"That's pretty bad," I agreed. "But his older brother's is worse. He has a ten-year-old Jeep that says I SPEED. Nice to be subtle. What a jerk."

"WAS HIS," said my mother suddenly. "When Bonnie's husband left her for another woman, she put a license plate on his pride and joy, an old Corvette, saying WAS HIS."

"That must've eaten his heart out," chuckled my father. "What about your cousin Phil? His license plate's in pretty bad taste."

"Why? GUTBUSTR's in bad taste for a gastroenterologist?" she said, pretending indignation.

We all laughed.

"What about those people down the block from Grandma, the ones with the new Mercedes?" I said. "I can't make up my mind whether theirs is clever or tacky."

"Well, the car was a gift from her husband on their fortieth wedding anniversary," said my mother, "and he gave her the car with the plate already on it. It would be a bit much for me, but the idea was kind of sweet."

"What does it say?" asked Allison impatiently.

"HERCEDES," I said, in my best imitation of a hushed tone.

"Come on, honey, that's nothing. This could be your HERCURY," said my father, of the seven-year-old station wagon we were riding in.

My mom groaned as she leaned over and squeezed his thigh. "Thanks, but I think 3-4-4 U-K-Z kind of fits me."

It was quiet for a moment as each of us tried to come up with another witty traveling billboard.

"Oh," said Allison, with a look that promised whatever she'd just remembered would be more interesting than any vanity plate. She pulled back her long, curly black hair and made a ponytail with the purple scrunchy that had been waiting on her wrist for just a moment. Her large brown eyes, rimmed with copper eye shadow, looked up into her head. "I can't believe I forgot to tell you. Do you want to hear the sickest thing?"

"Of course," I said, sitting up taller, hoping that it was something I hadn't heard already.

"You know Diane, the sophomore with the bad perm who wears those hideous press-on fingernails?"

I knew her as Diane with four holes in each

ear who looked amazing in her black spandex leggings. "Yeah, she was in my math class last year."

"Did you know her parents were getting a divorce?"

Another divorce was scarcely big news in my neighborhood. "What about it?"

"It's the best story. Her dad teaches in the same high school in Queens as my cousin Roberta. She says he's been having an affair with the dance teacher for months. Well, last week when he was getting undressed, Diane's mom saw *writing* on his *butt*."

"Writing on his butt?"

"Uh-huh. Like initials and hearts and people's names but all backward like you'd see them in a mirror."

"Backward writing on his behind?"

"I didn't get it at first either. You'll never guess how it got there," said Allison, gloating.

"So *tell* me." It was really annoying the way she dragged out a story. Till you almost didn't care anymore.

"I hate when people gossip, especially at the expense of other people's misery," interrupted my ethically scrupulous mom. As editor of a local women's monthly newsletter, she was always the champion of the injured party, the defender of the underdog—no matter what

4

the issue. And she was passionate about any cause lucky enough to stir her sympathies. My dad swore she was a nun in a former life. He made fun of her, teasing about things like taxes, where he always threatened to tell less than the whole truth about expenses and stuff. But you knew down deep he really liked her that way.

All of a sudden he hooted. "I've got it. Don't tell me the poor bastard was sitting on a desk with his pants down. . . ."

"Stephen!" exclaimed my mother after she inhaled sharply. Then she punched his arm.

Allison seemed a little taken aback that her delicious tidbit was now being digested four ways. It bothered her less that my mother disapproved of her telling the story than it did that my father enjoyed it so much! Also I don't think her dad says words like "bastard" in front of her. She turned red and whispered, "He's right. They were doing it on a desk in one of the classrooms after school. And the writing on the desk . . ."

The whole idea just grossed me out. Two teachers, *any* two teachers I ever knew, doing it at all, let alone in a school, extramaritally, on a desk I might sit at the next morning was more than I could handle.

"Does Diane know all this?"

"If we know, I'm sure she knows," answered Allison smugly.

"And her mom's divorcing him?"

"Uh-huh."

"I hope she never finds out we know," I said, surprising myself with how bad I felt for Diane. I brushed my bangs out of my eyes and inspected my straight blond hair for split ends. This was my new habit of choice to distract myself whenever an unpleasant thought made me uncomfortable. It replaced cleaning my always mysteriously smudged tortoiseshell glasses. Or counting my freckles. Or doing isometric exercises to firm up my thighs.

"She won't, if you don't tell her," said Allison. She looked more than a little disappointed with my reaction to her hot news.

I was glad we were going to Edgemont. Sometimes it was nice to get away from the North Shore and the pressures of comparing grades and vacations and how sun-bleached and curly your hair was. A few girls couldn't understand why I'd look forward to spending part of Christmas vacation at a summer cottage. It was OK in the warm weather, but they wanted to be in places with names like Paradise Island and Ixtapa during winter vacation. These were the girls who replaced their Keds when they got dirty instead of putting them in the washing machine, the ones who bought Justin cowboy boots to match one particular sweater. Let them go to the beach and lie there bored for hours each day risking skin cancer and third-degree burns just to come back to school with a tan, I thought. I knew Allison and I would have a better time.

The car sped away along the almost deserted roads. Allison took out the prom preview issue of *Seventeen*, tucked her legs under her, and was gone into the world of white strapless gowns and sleek black limos. Dad was singing along to one of those fifties tunes on the golden oldies station I let him listen to for at least a half hour of the ride. Mom was scribbling on one of the hundreds of pads she keeps wherever she is—jotting down endless lists of article ideas, of things we need at the supermarket, of tomorrow's chores. It's a habit she insists would lessen my stress and anxiety if I would adopt it. But a glimpse of her on a day when she's misplaced her notepad convinces me she's not quite the poster child for Life Under Control.

We were going to meet the Schumans in Edgemont. Raymond Schuman was my dad's best friend. For the past few years he had also been his boss—he'd gotten him a job as the assistant commissioner of procurement for student loans for New York State after Dad's office supply business went bankrupt. Uncle Ray himself was kind of famous in the state government. He was often quoted in the newspaper, and sometimes I'd see him on TV standing next to the governor. He and my father had been best friends for as long as I could remember. Dad's life had definitely improved since he started working for the government. He wore his hair longish now and even though he was still fifty pounds too heavy, he seemed more confident. I knew Dad loved his job and the fact that he didn't have to worry about paying the rent on a store or how many customers wouldn't show up if it rained.

He and Uncle Ray spent hours on the phone, sometimes for business, mostly just laughing. They even scheduled their haircuts and tennis lessons at the same time. Ten years before, they bought these adjoining cottages on the bay and our families had been spending summers and winter weekends together ever since.

Uncle Ray and his wife, Carole, had two daughters, eighteen and nineteen, and even though they tended to ignore me most of the time, I loved listening to what I thought of as coming attractions of what life had in store. They always were halfway decent to me because they liked my brother. Matt was a junior at Johns Hopkins. This was the first Christmas he wouldn't be coming with us—which was why I invited Allison.

Not that Matt spent that much time with me anyway. Most of the time he acted like he was forty, not just four years older than me. My parents always said he seemed to know exactly where he was going from age six on. Part of me admired that. I mean, I'll never see grades like his, or spend my summers volunteering to teach kids in the inner city to read, or wear Salvation Army clothes, or be a doctor. My mom once said, "I think Matt keeps a lot of stuff bottled up. I bet he secretly wishes he could yell and laugh and cry and react as honestly as you do. He pays a price for his success. Remember, nobody has it all." I had long given up on the fantasy of being on cozy, intimate terms with him, but I was still really proud he was my brother.

"How long till we're there?" asked Allison. I looked out the window at the lifeless vineyards, cornfields, and potato farms.

"Another half hour or so," I said.

"Is your place like that?" she asked, pointing to an old, well-tended, impressive-looking clapboard farmhouse along the road.

"Nah. Our place is a small cottage, not a

house." I hoped for the tenth time since I asked her that Allison was not going to be dreadfully disappointed when we arrived. Once, when we had gone to Soho for the day, I told her that the fifties look she admired reminded me of our place on the Jersey Shore. Allison was excited about seeing thirty-five-year-old furnishings—the ones she'd seen on the old black-and-white episodes of *Ozzie and Harriet*—in living color. I thought about our marbleized yellow Formica kitchen counter and red oilcloth, the twelve-inch TV on its brass stand, piled high with old magazines, on an oval, braided brown area rug. I promised her she'd never seen anything like our BarcaLounger in a Liberty Bell motif or the stained, faded print of the Degas ballet dancers. I had to admit these things sounded a lot more quaint and appealing in memory than they were in real life.

I described my room on the closed-in porch as "facing the bay," a fact she'd find infinitely more exciting in the summer when there were motorboats and waterskiing and dune buggies and bonfires. She hardly believed me when I told her that we always ate in the Main Street Diner and ordered blueberry cheesecake just to watch our waitress run down the block to the supermarket, buy an Entenmann's cake, run back to the kitchen, and present us a huge slice with coffee—all within five minutes. I might've oversold its exotic nature just a bit with a mostly made-up description of Edgemont's two gorgeous churches and three-hundred-year-old cemeteries, but I really wanted her to come with me and I had been sure Melissa was going to ask her to visit her grandmother in Boca Raton. Anyway, now that we were getting closer, I was beginning to get nervous.

All of a sudden we heard a phone ring in the car. It was Dad's brand-new Christmas present from Uncle Ray. Mom—a graduate of the Frugal School of Cheapness, who counted the sheets of Viva paper towels we used, always kept and reheated the leftover white rice from take-out Chinese food, and squirted sparing amounts of window washer fluid to clean her windshield—thought his gift was ridiculously extravagant and impractical. Dad, ever the sport, loved spending whatever he had, mostly on us. I knew nothing gave him more pleasure than throwing a twenty-dollar bill into my bag every once in a while when Mom wasn't around. He loved the attention he got when he walked into the few local restaurants we go to, after slipping the maître d' some money to "expedite matters." I think the few arguments my parents ever had were about whether money is to be spent or saved.

"Can I answer the phone?" I knew it had to be Uncle Ray since he was the only one who had the number. "He's probably there already and wants us to pick something up on the way."

"Sure, hon, just press down this button."

"Doesn't it cost you a fee every time you receive a call?" whispered my mom as I reached over the front seat to pick up the receiver.

"This is Stephen Gresham's private traveling secretary speaking. Can I help you?"

"Erika, is that you?"

I was glad Allison was there to see me talking this way to Raymond Schuman. "Yes, Uncle Ray. What do you need—Mallomars? Dove-Bars? Toilet paper?"

"Erika, let me speak to Daddy," he said flatly, ignoring me completely. It wasn't like him. He was like my fairy godfather, I would tease him, when he'd mail me two tickets on the floor of the Coliseum to see Billy Joel or get us all the best seats for the U.S. Open. He used to come by when I was little just to take me for ice cream in his limo. Sometimes, I had to admit, he was a bit too loud and acted a little too impressed with himself, but it seemed like a small price to pay for the magic of the rest. I knew he liked the fact that I was a good athlete and that I wasn't intimidated by all the fuss around him and that I always laughed at his gross jokes.

"Dad, it's grumpy, cranky, mean old Uncle Ray," I said, loud enough for him to hear, as I handed the phone to my father. It was set on speakerphone so we all could hear the conversation.

"Hey, Ray, what's up?" The joke in my family was always, If Ray and my mom were on a sinking ship, my Dad wouldn't know who to save first.

"Where are you now?"

"On Route Forty-six, about twenty minutes away from the house. When did you get there?"

"I'm home. You better turn around and head back right away."

My mother looked sharply at my father. She put her pen in her pocketbook.

"What's wrong?" my dad asked, sounding like someone was choking him. I couldn't see his face, but I could hear the panic in his voice.

"It's over. I just got a call. They know."

"Wait, wait," my dad said as he fumbled with the buttons of his new toy, trying to shut off the speaker. "Just calm down. I'm going to pull over, get out of the car, and talk to you.

Just calm down." He spoke extra slow and very quietly like he was talking a small child out of a bad dream.

My mother didn't say a word. She just stared at my father's face. He wouldn't look at her, but I could see he was pretending that the difficulty of trying to find a place to stop while talking on the phone gave him no opportunity to return her glance.

"The slimeball from Chicago, that Baker guy. He's trying to save his ass. He figured he'd give 'em something to chew on . . ."

"Ray, you're on the speakerphone. Just hold on till I park," said my dad in a voice the police would use to talk someone out of jumping off a ledge.

But Uncle Ray just ignored him. "They know everything. We're finished. The cash, the stock, the contracts, everything. We're talking federal here, eight and a half to twenty-five. God, the press is going to eat this up. It's over, old buddy." Then he started to sob.

"I'll call you back," said my father, and he slammed down the phone. There were beads of sweat forming above his mustache. I tried to focus on the expression on his face in the rearview mirror. It looked like one of those models you see who stand absolutely still, not even blinking, for hours, so that you can't tell if they're alive or not.

The car was completely silent. We all looked straight ahead. Allison sneezed.

"God bless you," my mother and I chanted at the same time.

What kept me from throwing up was an old trick my father taught me from a stress management course he'd once taken.

"Whenever you're stressed out," he'd said, "just inhale deeply to the count of four and exhale fully through your mouth to the count of four. Do that fifteen times slowly and you'll regulate your thermostat." I tried it a few times—before my last tennis tournament, after a fight with Allison, the morning of my math Regents exams. It seemed to work, probably because I was too busy counting and breathing to worry. I prayed that it would work now.

My father pulled over near a small deserted pond. It was 4:30 and just beginning to get dark. I looked out into the cold, gray fog lying over the water and thought if this were being filmed, the director couldn't ask for better weather. My father grabbed the phone and walked about a quarter way around the pond to an empty bench. We saw him dial and then start talking.

My mother opened the car door. She glanced back, torn for a second between protecting us and running to listen to that phone conversation. I knew what she'd decide.

"I'm going to sit with Daddy. I have no idea what this is all about, but I'm sure that once it's explained to us it'll seem a lot less serious than it does right now. Just sit tight. I'll be back in a few minutes."

As soon as she slammed the door, Allison asked, "What do you think is going on? Does this mean we're not going to Edgemont? Are you scared?"

Scared I could have handled. Scared was uncomfortable, but at least it was familiar. I think what I was feeling was devastated. My grandma used that word all the time to describe how she felt when her brother died, or when Grandpa's business burned down and they couldn't pay the mortgage. Europe was devastated after World War II. Los Angeles after the earthquake. And me, right then.

I looked at my father hunched over the phone, one hand covering his free ear to help him hear over the wind. My mother sat a few inches away, just looking at his face. What could Uncle Ray mean—"We're finished. It's over. They know everything"? I forced my eyes away from them and looked around the pond. There were several trees evenly spaced around the water, their skinny, naked branches sadly swaying in the wind. Then I saw the Christmas tree. There in the middle of the pond, looking full, hearty, and healthy, was a huge spruce, lights and all, complete with an enormous star on top. It wasn't lit yet, and I forced my mind to figure out how they got the tree out there and how they would light it without getting electrocuted. It was the kind of question the four of us normally would have loved to tackle. Dad would have come up with some supernatural solution, Mom would have been totally practical, Matt would have gotten into the technical logistics of the lights and how they worked. And I—Ugh! It was a stupid game.

"What time is it?" Allison asked.

"Four forty-five," I answered, suddenly aware that my father was no longer talking on the phone. He and my mother sat bent over, elbows on their thighs, staring down at the ground. Only my dad's lips were moving. After a few minutes my mother stood up and started to walk back to the car. My father quickly followed her. He tried to grab her hand, but she had jammed it deep inside her coat. He walked a step or two behind her, talking all the time. Her eyes never left the ground.

It just wasn't possible. He'd come into the car and clear up the confusion. This was Daddy, who'd never missed one of my tennis matches in three years. Who made my lunch every day. When I was little, the only father in our neighborhood to put on a costume and take his child trick-or-treating. Careful Daddy, who never even got a speeding ticket, who wouldn't sign a note to excuse me from gym when I was unprepared because it would "lead to bad habits."

The two car doors opened at the same time. Both of them sat down stiffly as if their backs hurt. The moment my father started the car, the lights on the Christmas tree went on. We all saw what ordinarily would have been an extraordinary sight, and no one said a word. I couldn't wait to get out of there.

"I'm sorry, girls, we're going to have to go home. I'll make it up to you, I promise." My dad sounded more distracted than sorry.

"Allison, you're welcome to stay over for a few days, and we'll see what we can do to salvage this week. Maybe a walk down Columbus Avenue, or we'll check out what's playing at Radio City."

Radio City? Now I knew Mom was operating on automatic pilot. She'd lost it. The

Christmas show at Radio City was for eight-year-olds and tourists. If she were in her right mind instead of the Twilight Zone, she'd know I thought going to Radio City belonged on David Letterman's list of the ten dorkiest things to do over Christmas vacation. Besides, how was I ever going to find out what was going on if Allison was around?

"Oh, I have an idea, girls," Mom continued on, way too brightly. "There's an exhibit of women's tennis memorabilia at the Queens Tennis Complex. It's supposed to be really interesting. Two tennis players like yourselves might find it fascinating."

Poor Mom. Just because we played the game didn't mean we cared about Billie Jean King's first racket. She'd have known that under normal circumstances. Like a half hour ago.

I was relieved to hear Allison refuse, giving some phony excuse about needing the opportunity to get started on her social studies paper anyway. No one was saying anything vaguely resembling what they were thinking. We were all just concentrating on pushing back the tension, trying to survive the two-hour ride home. I never realized how much mindless time polite conversation could take up. I half heard my mother offering us an apple and Allison offering me Life Savers and her most recent copies of *Seventeen* and *YM* to browse through.

I felt like somebody had died. I wondered if it would be Stephen Gresham's butt the school would be talking about when we got back from vacation. I watched the back of my father's shoulders lift and fall as he practiced his deep breathing.

CHAPTER 2

New York Daily Mirror

State investigators removed files and changed the lock yesterday at the office of Stephen Gresham, the Assistant Commissioner of Procurement for Student Loans, after officials provided them with information about the possibility of improprieties at the agency.

The state revealed it was cooperating with a federal inquiry into the possibility that bribes had been paid to state officials. Mr. Gresham, who is 48 years old and lives on Long Island, called in sick on Monday and again yesterday. He did not return several telephone calls to his home seeking comment.

ONE THING I'll say for my father. He didn't stall, he didn't beat around the bush or try to justify himself with excuses and alibis.

"I didn't go looking for it. It happened," he began.

The three of us were sitting at the kitchen table the morning after the silent drive back from Edgemont. I wasn't happy with the way this conversation was starting. What I wanted to hear was that this whole thing wasn't as bad as it appeared. No way was I prepared for a list of troubles that would take forever to get better. I was afraid of what he might tell me.

Dad's face looked like a room where the only light had been turned off.

The night before, I had gone straight upstairs and put on my stereo as loud as I could get away with.

"We'll talk in the morning," he'd called up after me, while my mother put up a pot of coffee, signifying a long night ahead for both of them. I was glad to postpone the dreaded truth for at least a few more hours. A few more hours of my good old reliable boring life. I couldn't remember what had been bothering me earlier in the day. One thing about major trouble—it blows the small stuff so far away it's barely worth worrying about.

I got up early that morning, calming myself with MTV's *House of Style* and Froot Loops. Now I searched my mother's face as she busied herself folding laundry. She had positioned herself at the far end of the large oval dining room table. Everything of consequence was discussed here. We used the table mostly at holidays or celebrating birthdays and terrific report cards. Or deciding what color to paint the outside of the house or what colleges to apply to. Sitting there at breakfast made the occasion seem especially ominous. My mother's face showed nothing.

"Some of us are lucky in life to have just the temptation but not the opportunity to take advantage of certain situations," my dad continued, sweeping his middle finger along the table to pick up the stray sesame seeds that had fallen off the bagel he'd eaten for breakfast. I noticed that his finger must have been damp to so successfully clean up his area in so few trips across.

He was obviously uneasy. He kept clearing his throat of a tickle I was sure didn't exist. The three of us sitting so far apart around a table that comfortably seats twelve, made me feel like we were in one of those old movies about a very rich, very cold society family. All that was missing was a maid to come bustling out of the kitchen to ask if we wanted to heat up our coffee.

"You understand, Erika, what my job entails. That it's my responsibility to go after people who borrowed money from New York State to help them pay their tuition while they're in college. They sign an agreement that after they graduate they will pay back this loan at a certain low percentage of interest. Well, for hundreds of thousands of young people, returning money they owe is not high on their list of priorities. Their debt runs way up into the hundreds of millions of dollars. And I'm the head of the agency in charge of collecting this money. Do you understand so far?"

Yeah, Dad, I thought. Now stop talking like I'm a stranger. I know what you do for a living. My heart started to beat so fast and so loud. I tried to catch my mother's eye, but she avoided my glance, meticulously piling up the towels in the laundry basket.

"Uh-huh," I answered, starting to get fidgety. "Now can you get to the point? What was Uncle Ray so upset about yesterday?" I knew I sounded mean, but I was trying to harden myself for the horrible part I knew was coming.

"Here's where things get sticky," he plowed on. "In order to go after all this money, I hire a firm called a collection agency. They track down these scofflaws by sending them letter after letter and hounding them until they agree to some kind of payment plan. The agency's fee is a percentage of the money they collect." He stopped for a second, wiped his upper lip with a napkin, then continued. "You know that expression 'It's all who you know'? Well, politics works with that as its theme song."

"Stephen," my mother interrupted, "a simple explanation of what happened will suffice. It's not necessary to give Erika a political science lesson in the ways of the world at this point." She pursed her lips.

"All right, Charlotte. I'm doing the best I can. This isn't easy, you know."

There was something in the whininess of his tone that made her sit up straight. She raised her eyebrows.

"Really," she said. Her tone was icy.

Dad's face flushed. I stared at his knee jumping up and down, a habit of his I'd notice when he watched the Knicks play or when a waiter took a ridiculously long time to bring us our food.

"OK. Many collection agencies would love to have the job. They could make a fortune if they do their job well. And many different agencies could do it well." His voice got very low. "I made an arrangement with one particular agency. To show their appreciation for being chosen for the job, they paid me and Uncle Ray a small fee. Someone in that agency was just arrested for selling cocaine. In order to get

his sentence reduced, he told the author-
ities about the arrangement his company had
with me."

"Is that under-the-table money?" I asked,
suddenly remembering an expression my
grandpa used when he told me about how soda
companies and candy suppliers would pay him
to carry their products in his candy store years
ago.

"That's one way of putting it," my father
said quietly, a weak smile tugging at his mouth.

"But Grandpa was responsible only to himself," my mom said sharply. "Your father is a
civil servant who works for the government.
When he takes money, he's betraying the public trust."

"So what did Uncle Ray mean, 'It's all
over'? Why did we have to come home?" If it
was just about this "under-the-table" stuff, that
didn't sound like the end of the world.

"The charges are serious, Erika. You're going to be hearing words like 'bribery' and 'kickbacks.' There's going to be a lot of attention
focused on us for a while. The newspapers and
TV stations will all want to ask questions. I'm
depending on you to be very mature."

"Mature?" His preachy tone totally annoyed me. "How do I act mature about something like this?" He does something illegal and

I have to be mature? "Where's the money now? Why don't you just give it back?"

My father didn't answer.

"Can't you hire a lawyer to explain that it was a mistake? That you didn't realize . . . ?"

My mom answered for him. "It was a mistake, all right. A very big mistake your father made. One that we're all going to have to pay for. He realized what he was doing. That's why we didn't know anything about it." She picked up the laundry basket to bring upstairs.

My father looked after her as she walked away. He slumped down in his chair.

"I'm going to ask you to do something very hard now, honey," he said. "You're going to be hearing all kinds of stories about Uncle Ray and me. Don't be angry with people for believing rumors—it's human nature to gloat over someone else's misfortune. Just, please"—his voice cracked—"don't act like a victim. Hold your head up. *You've* done nothing wrong."

The more pitiful he looked, the angrier I felt. "Why did you get involved with this guy, Dad? Did you hide all the money? What's going to happen to you?"

"Don't badger me, Erika," my dad answered abruptly, standing up to signal the discussion was closed. "I need you on my side now. When I know more, we'll talk again."

"I'm trying to be on your side, Dad, but it's hard. What if I told you I was caught cheating on my SATs? Or the attendance officer called and said I hadn't been in school for two weeks? You might be on my side, but you'd be asking me plenty of questions."

"You couldn't begin to understand . . . ," my father said.

"Try me."

"Another time. I have to go lie down. I didn't sleep very well last night."

"You wouldn't let me get away with a lame excuse like that," I muttered. "That's what people say when they can't tell the truth, when they need time to make the facts more presentable."

"Hey!" my father barked. "I'm still your father. Have some respect for what I say."

"Then talk to me," I pleaded.

Without another word he turned away from the table, went upstairs to his study, and closed the door.

"I'm going over to Grandma's house," said my mother, coming down the steps with the empty basket. "The sooner I tell them all this, the better. I don't want them finding out on the evening news." She hurriedly put on her coat.

For a second I saw her running to her mother, to get a hug and some words to make things better. I wished she could stay home with me.

"Are you all right?" she asked, feeling around her pocket for her car keys.

"I think so. My stomach feels a little queasy. How about you?" I really hoped she'd sit down next to me and talk. Give me some idea of the damage I could expect from this catastrophe. Comfort me—even if she had to lie.

"Make yourself a cup of tea," she said without hearing me, and she was gone.

Reassure Daughter, I guess, was not on her list of morning activities.

I sat at the dining room table for almost an hour. My family was going to be famous. It had always been my dream to be a name on everyone's lips. Only my scenarios were much different. I used to think about what I'd say to reporters if a plane landed in my backyard, or if that weird guy who hangs around Waldbaums turned out to be a sniper who mowed down ten people shopping in Roosevelt Field.

Or I'd win ten million dollars in the lottery, playing my math test grades for that quarter. My hair would come out great that day, I'd hold my stomach in, and I'd give a brilliant interview. "I never thought I'd be so happy to get a fifty-four on a quiz," I'd say with a sunny smile.

In my favorite there's my face on the cover of *Seventeen* as one of the top five high school tennis players in the country. My eyes would be sparkling, exactly the same shade of blue as the sky behind me. There'd be a photo layout inside with captions explaining how my awesome tennis ability and American beauty looks won't deter me from my goal of becoming a pediatrician. "Stay in school," I'd say to my adoring adolescent public. "A good education is essential for whatever you do in life . . ."

The phone rang, forcing me back to the dining room table. It was Allison.

"Are you OK?" she asked. "What's up?"

There was something in her "What's up?" I didn't like.

"I'm OK. I'm busy right now. Can I call you back later?"

"Sure. Oh, my mom just wanted you to tell your mom how sorry she was about . . . everything."

"Uh, OK. I'll tell her." I wondered how Allison had possibly explained what happened. And why her mother was sending condolences to my mom. No one had died.

"She said if your mom wanted to talk, she should call her anytime." There was a tone in Allison's voice, like when she found out Julie's uncle had AIDS: all concerned and helpful on the outside but all curious for the gory details underneath.

"Thanks," I said shortly. "Listen, Allison, I'd appreciate if you didn't tell anyone about yesterday until I figure out what to say."

There was silence on the other end.

I was too late.

"Gee, I'm sorry, Erika. I spoke to Ingrid and Laura last night when I got home . . ."

"What did you say?!" I said angrily. "You don't even know anything. What did you say!" If Ingrid and Laura knew, for sure half the junior class did, too.

"Take it easy. Why are you so mad?" said Allison. "I had to explain why I was home. I just said your father got into some kind of trouble with the law. That's right, isn't it?"

"Yeah, that's right," I spit out. "Now if you can keep yourself from appearing on *Hard Copy*, that would be great. You're supposed to be my best friend."

"I am, I am," protested Allison. "What did I do? Do you really think you can keep this a secret? My father said anything involving Raymond Schuman is going to make headlines. You have to face it, Erika, everyone's going to know anyway."

"OK, but you don't have to help it along." After a few seconds I added, "I'm mad, but not at you. I'm sorry . . . You called at exactly the wrong moment. I'll call you later." I hung up. I knew that as much as Allison cared about me, she loved being a source of hot gossip. This whole thing was going to be a severe test of her loyalty. And I wasn't at all convinced I'd be happy with the final grade.

I went upstairs to my room, flopped on my bed, and stared out the window, where five shades of gray outlined the sky and the tree branches moved slightly in the icy wind. Inside my room everything seemed cozy and familiar. The collage of Absolut ads on my door, the posters of Marilyn Monroe on the wall near my bed, the huge centerfold of Tom Cruise on my ceiling. This was reality. My room was in typical (for me) one-teensy-step-before-disaster shape, with wet towels draped over the desk chair I never sat in, a minimountain of dirty underwear and socks to go down the laundry chute, three glasses with remnants of diet Coke to be put in the dishwasher, empty hangers on the doorknob, five shoes on the floor.

The door creaked as Bailey gingerly made her way in. Bailey, my perceptually handicapped dog who specializes in walking into walls, chewing on shoelaces, and protecting me from mean-old-mister-middle-of-the-night when I go downstairs at 2:00 A.M. for a fix of Mallomars and milk, jumped up on my bed to cuddle. She'd known better than to hang around the dining room this morning.

Then I remembered the one person who would definitely relate to how I was feeling. I sat up and dialed Matt's number. He was at school working on a special project with his major professor. I hardly ever called him because he had this annoying way of making me feel that any time spent in conversation with me was a big favor. But today would be different. He would know how impossible it was for our dad—the guy who eats salami with melted Velveeta on a bagel, who mimics Jerry Lewis, who wouldn't even bet in a football pool—to be involved in such a predicament.

He picked up on the first ring.

"Hello." He sounded sleepy.

"Matt, hi—it's Erika. Did I wake you?" I hadn't realized it was 11:30, practically the crack of dawn in college standard time.

"Nah, that's OK. I figured I'd be hearing from you today. How'ya doing?"

"So you know," I said, relieved not to have to go through the whole story. I should have figured they'd called him last night. "Can you believe it?"

"Yeah, I believe it. I always thought that he and Ray with their manicures and fifty-dollar haircuts acted more like bad little boys than civil servants."

I couldn't believe what I was hearing. I knew Matt thought Ray's taste in jewelry, fancy restaurants, and custom-made suits was a bit much, but the bitterness in his voice cut right through me.

"I'm humiliated and disgusted more than I am surprised," he continued. "Corruption in government is something everyone takes for granted. I just wish my own father hadn't been so stupid."

"Did he explain all the facts to you? Do you know how he just got roped into—"

"Look, Erika—he could explain facts and numbers from today till doomsday. There's only one truth. He lied, he stole, and he got caught. I'm sorry I won't be there when the shit hits the fan, but I'm in the middle of organizing an off-campus soup kitchen for my junior thesis, and I can't come home."

"That's OK. I understand," I said. I wanted to get off the phone before I started to cry. I felt like I'd been slapped across the face. "You can call me anytime if you want to know what's going on."

"I will, Erika. How's tennis?"

He always asked me that whenever he felt the pressure to make conversation. Not that he ever really listened to the answer.

"We play for the county championship in six weeks."

"Hey, that's great."

"Uh-huh."

"Well, good luck. And say hi to Mr. DaMaio for me."

Mr. DaMaio was my tennis coach, who had been Matt's basketball coach when he was in school. He was tough but fair and somehow managed to make everyone on the team, from the best player to the worst, feel equally important. He probably was the one person Matt and I agreed about. I shuddered when I thought what his reaction to this mess would be.

I sat staring at the receiver after Matt hung up. Thanks for nothing, big brother.

"Come here, Bailey," I called, patting my bed. I hugged her, and she licked my face.

"Do you believe Matt?" I asked her. "He never once said the word *Dad*. For someone with a photographic memory he seems to have forgotten how he'd run to Uncle Ray to take out his splinters or to Dad to kiss his boo-boos. What a selfish creep!"

I got up to take a shower. The hot water

felt great, and I wound up staying under the showerhead much longer than usual. Most times I'm in and out in five minutes, but a day I didn't have the energy to face loomed ahead. I shut off the water, wrapped my head in a hundred-year-old Muppets towel, and bundled up in my ancient pink terry robe with the world's most strategically placed, embarrassing holes in it. I don't know how they happen, the holes you get in clothes you absolutely love to death, but my old bathrobe had some beauts. Vaguely I heard banging at the front door.

"Could you get that?" I yelled as I opened the door to the steamy bathroom. There was no answer. Mom must still be at Grandma's, and I certainly wasn't going to knock on Dad's closed door.

Someone had their annoying finger on the doorbell. *Dingdong. Dingdong. Dingdong.* The house was quiet and dark because Mom hadn't even opened the window shades this morning. I was sure it was Michael, the ten-year-old wheeler-dealer who lived down the block. He was always selling raffle tickets for the Boy Scouts, or else offering to wash our car. We used him to walk and feed Bailey when we went to the shore. He'd probably seen Dad's car and wanted to know why we were back.

"Who is it?" I asked, just checking that no

one more important than a ten-year-old would see me looking this divine. The doorbell stopped ringing. No one answered. I stood facing the door with my hand on the knob, ready to open it. Just then I saw a flashbulb go off right outside the living room window. The window was covered with beige, lacy drapes that were sort of see-through if you looked hard enough. Again a light flashed. I ducked under the windowsill and peered out through my still fogged up glasses. There was a young guy with a knapsack and a camera pressed right up to the window, not twelve inches from me.

"I don't know if any of these are going to come out," he said to a woman standing a few feet away at the front door.

"We can only do our best," she answered.

"I'm sure someone's home. Maybe the bell's not working."

She started banging again.

"What do you want?" I yelled, crawling back to the front door.

"Shhh," she said to the man with the camera. "I just want to ask you a few questions, that's all," the woman called to me. "What's your name, dear?"

"Who are you?" I answered in a tone to let her know I was not her "dear."

"My name is Fanny Gaynes. I'm a reporter for *Village Viewpoints*."

"What do you want?"

"Doesn't Stephen Gresham live here? Is it possible to have a word with him?"

"He's not home. Please go away," I said, suddenly panicked my mom would return and they'd take pictures of her.

"Just tell me, is Mr. Gresham your father? How is he handling the news of the impending investigation? Is he upset?"

What kind of question was that? All of a sudden he wasn't like everyone else? He was a criminal who took this kind of news like it happened all the time?

"I don't know what you're talking about. Please go away."

"Maybe he hasn't told her yet," I heard her whisper to the photographer. "We'll come back tomorrow when it's in the paper." She cleared her throat.

"OK, dear, we're leaving. Just tell your father we'll be back to talk to him tomorrow. Sorry to bother you."

They walked to an old dented yellow VW parked in front of the house. I watched them leave, glad to see the guy who was carrying all the photography equipment trip over the loose piece of slate on the walkway. I was calm till they pulled away. Then I felt myself trembling. I ran upstairs to my room, slammed the door shut, and dove onto my bed. Bailey woke up as the bed bounced up and down. Great job of protecting the house, dog. How scary that they already knew where we lived. What would they have thought if I'd opened the door and treated them to a glimpse of Muppet-toweled, holey bathrobed, moose-slippered me? What gave them the right to bang on people's doors like that?

I wondered whether my father had heard. I wondered how my mother was going to handle the news that they'd be back tomorrow. And most of all I wondered as I turned over in dire need of a glimpse of Tom Cruise, how I was going to survive going back to school next week.

CHAPTER 3

New York Tribune, *Editorial*

Stephen Gresham is being charged with extortion in what federal officials describe as a widening inquiry into thousands of dollars in bribes paid to state officials by private collection agencies. The state education scandal is ballooning into an illustration of the degradation of government.

ON THE DAY AFTER the story broke in the papers, my father had to go into Manhattan for the first of many fourteen-hour days to answer questions asked by the federal prosecutors. Knowing there'd be photographers all over the place and not wanting to look like a drug dealer walking in with a jacket over his head, he'd rummaged through the top of the hall closet looking for a hat or some sunglasses to hide behind. Down tumbled two old umbrellas, a few stray gloves, some scarves, and a rain hat—

as my grandmother would say—from the year one.

"Charlotte, where are those big glasses, the ones we bought a few years ago when we went skiing?"

"It's not that sunny today, Stephen," my mother answered dryly.

"I know. I'd just like to cover my eyes," he mumbled, not looking at either of us and starting to throw back the stuff that had fallen down.

"They're in a shopping bag filled with the rest of the ski stuff, in the back of the closet," Mom offered flatly. Any other time she would've helped him, but now she sat sipping her coffee, watching him on his hands and knees in the foyer.

"Are you sure you want to wear those glasses? They're kind of big on you," she finally said when he found them.

He wound up getting photographed from every angle in those ridiculously large sunglasses. In some pictures he just looked silly, but in most he looked miserable, evil, mean. Like a hit man. From that day on, whenever there was an article about the scandal or an update on the evening news, there was Stephen Gresham, the short, pudgy bad guy with the humongous sunglasses.

A terrible numbness invaded my body. It was the only way I could handle the way the press massacred him. One day they commented on his $500 suit. My father never spent that kind of money on clothes. That suit was a Syms special, marked down to $159, that my mother had bought him last fall. The *Tribune* wrote that we lived in Roslyn Estates, an exclusive development in the same zip code but completely different in income level. The *News* said we had three cars; we had two. It wouldn't have served their purpose to say that one was five years old and the other seven years old, so they didn't. Our Edgemont bungalow became a "beachfront summer home." My brother, scholarshipped and student loaned to his eyeballs, attended an "exclusive private university." Any way they could make us look rich and greedy, they did.

Newspapers were very big on facts. I just thought they had to be true.

My friends at school tried to be sympathetic, but I could see they were too enthralled with the gossip angle to offer any comfort.

"Do you think it's a good idea to keep reading the newspapers every night?" Allison asked a few days later, watching me chew on the same piece of apple over and over again at lunch in the cafeteria. "I mean, it's not like you're gonna find out good news about your dad."

"Could *you* stop reading if it were *your* father?" I answered. "It's like picking a scab or biting down on a toothache; I can't help it."

I didn't mention that I hadn't slept more than four hours a night for the last week. A whole new routine began at 11:30 when I shut off the lights. First I waited for my head to stop pounding. Then when it didn't, I got up around midnight and took two aspirin. By 1:00 A.M. I'd drift off, till, like clockwork, I'd dream I was falling down a huge flight of stairs. My muscles tightened as I prepared to collide with the bottom of the stairwell. My eyes would fly open, my body would still be rigid, and I'd be covered with sweat. Now it was 2:15. Sometimes I felt like waking up was as bad as hitting bottom. At least then I'd be out cold.

"I couldn't believe how they described that plastic pool of yours, as a 'backyard complete with pool,'" said Ingrid, continuing to dissect yesterday's article. "Your overgrown wading pool sounded like one of those Hollywood heart-shaped deals."

Everyone laughed.

"It's really not funny," I said. "You know my

dad. He's as much of a gangster as Mr. Murphy." Mr. Murphy was our nerdy chemistry teacher.

"Relax, Erika," said Laura. I could see she was trying to be supportive. "Look, we like your dad, no matter what he did. He deals with politicians, right? So which one of them is lily-white enough to cast the first stone? It's not like he murdered anybody."

I sighed. She really thought she was making me feel better. Differentiating between my father and molesters and killers. It's like saying for a fat guy he didn't sweat much.

My head started to ache. I stood up and gathered my things.

"Where are you going?" asked Allison. "There's ten more minutes till the end of the period."

"I'm going to pick up a cartridge for my word processor," I lied. "I have a history paper due Thursday." I just had to get away from the table.

"OK," said Allison, not believing a word. "I'll speak to you later."

I knew once I left the table she'd hold court, doling out any scraps of information I might have told her that the rest didn't know yet. Some friend! Some people live for this stuff. She should thank my father for her sudden rise in popularity.

Me, I hated being so conspicuous. I walked through the halls feeling like I was dressed in fluorescent neon.

"Don't be so paranoid," my mother had said that morning. "How many kids in school read the paper or listen to the news anyway?"

It might've been only two or three, but they made sure everyone else knew what they learned. Even the dirtbags, the boys who cut class to smoke pot, who drove cars without mufflers, and who looked like they never washed their long, stringy hair or their Metallica T-shirts, knew what was going on.

"Hey, Erika, how's it going?" one of them asked, leaning against someone else's car, smoking a cigarette, as I walked out of school at three o'clock. "It's a shame your dad got caught. He wasn't doing nothing all those guys ain't been doin' for years. He just wasn't lucky, is all."

I had gone to school with these boys since kindergarten, but I don't think we'd talked since sixth grade. Now, because my father was being indicted, they wanted to be my friends. They felt sorry for him. Thought he was getting a raw deal. Maybe they and Laura could start a Stephen Gresham fan club. Maybe my dad could be the next model for No Excuses jeans.

Those creeps were better than the others, who just stared. Like I was guilty, too. It didn't make a difference if they were jocks or brains, skateboarders or hippy granolas, I was now much more interesting than I had been last semester. What a screwed-up world.

"Hey, wait up," said a voice behind me.

It was Russ Bianco, twin of Johnny Depp, drummer in the coolest high school band in Nassau County, star of many of my fantasies.

"You're Erika Gresham, right?" He fell in step beside me, and I instantly forgot where I was going. Nothing like a little sex appeal to chase away any remnants of rational thought.

"Uh-huh." I was torn between being thrilled he knew my name and being panicked that I had no idea how I was going to stay conscious.

"You live on Dogwood Road? The beige-and-brown house?"

I nodded. He knew where I lived! How could that possibly be bad?

"My older brother used to hang with your brother once in a while. I remember him. Always organizing those food drives, right? Real admirable-type guy."

"Uh-huh. He's very admirable." It was impossible to be funny or cute or anything approaching appealing till I had a clue where this conversation was going.

I glanced up at his face and tried to remember every detail to tell Allison later. Diamond stud earring. Smelled of Egoïste. Grungy in a careful, Ralph Lauren way. Suddenly he looked right into my eyes and smiled.

"You have freckles. I think they're so cute. When I was little, I used to call them sprinkles." He stopped walking and pulled me over to the wall. "Could I ask you a question?"

I was grateful for something to lean against.

"Sure," I said, smiling right back at him. At least I hadn't said *uh-huh* again.

"I know a lot of the media's been by your house lately 'cause I watch the evening news." He said it proudly, like it was some kind of intellectual feat. "I hope you don't think I'm out of line here, but I was wondering if, like, the next time Chuck Ruden came by, you know, the Long Island correspondent for channel two? You could maybe mention me and the band. Just, like, I'm your friend, and maybe he could come down sometimes and hear us play . . . I hear he's a really nice guy and into our kind of sound."

I didn't answer. What a jerk. Him. Me.

All my senses returned at once. "Yeah, OK," I said, moving away.

"It was hard for me, man, just coming up to you, out of the blue like this, but we got this agent now. And he keeps telling us to use all our connections. And I thought, a sweet kid like you . . . maybe you'd be willing to help us out . . ." He was still smiling, but now I noticed he had tuna fish on his breath.

"And your name again is . . . ?" I asked, innocently, sweet kid that I was.

"Oh, Russ Bianco," he said, suddenly confused. "I'm sorry, I thought you'd know."

"Well, I know now, Russ, and I'll keep you in mind if I ever meet up with Mr. Ruden."

I turned away and walked up the first staircase I came to. When I reached the first landing, I realized my nails were digging into my palms. I wished I could haul off and smash a tennis ball across court. Or scream. Or at least explain to everyone at school that what was happening in my house was not exciting . . . or cool . . . or anything but hideous.

That night I refused to be terrorized by the same nightmare. Happy thoughts, think happy thoughts, I repeated to myself. I once read that if you focus on something good, something pleasurable before you sleep, you can continue the story in your dreams. Pictures of successful tennis matches, of last Christmas at the shore, of my sweet-sixteen party flashed across my mind. I rejected each one as soon as my father's smiling face appeared. Then it hit me: the stuff sweet dreams are made of—my last day of camp last summer.

Greg Paskoff and I had been going to Camp Birchwood since we were ten. We usually wound up on the same color war team, and for the last two years we had written the alma mater together. As the only two in camp who really appreciated alternative music, we spent time together listening to each other's tapes and making fun of people who thought our taste too funky.

Greg was different from the other boys. He seemed to be totally unconscious of how he looked. We started out the same height, but now he was a tall, tan five feet eleven inches. He came to camp always needing a haircut, and during the summer his thick, dark, curly hair made its way down his neck and over his eyes. By the end of August he was borrowing my scrunchies to keep it back in a ponytail. Greg's smiling eyes, the color of the lake at noon, were his best feature. Although the small dimple (which he called a dent) in his left cheek was a close contender. Maybe because he paid it no mind, I never noticed, till that last day, how cute he really was.

Greg had a cutting sense of humor, but he never made jokes at someone else's expense. He was never embarrassed to play tennis with me, even though I was a much better player. He wasn't ashamed to say his favorite TV show of all time was *The Wonder Years*, or that he cried at the end of *The Last of the Mohicans*.

And he wasn't at all shy, that last day of camp, about letting me know that things between us were changing.

"Greg likes you," Becky, one of my eight-year-old campers, said as I was helping her close her trunk before loading it on the bus. "He always looks at you when you walk away from him."

"And that means he likes me? Maybe he just likes that I'm going."

"Uh-huh, if you saw him looking you'd see," she said dreamily. It was a new thought for me: Greg as more than a friend. Interesting.

It was about three o'clock when the last bus of kids left camp. My parents were coming to pick me up around six, on their way home from a week's vacation in New Hampshire.

About five o'clock Greg peeked his head in

my bunk. "You want to go for one last swim?" he asked with a smile.

It was a long-standing joke between us. I couldn't swim. Putting my face in the water just freaked me out. There was something about the coordination or holding my breath or some weird demon under the water that kept me dog-paddling six summers in a row. It was embarrassing, but at least it was a fault Greg had known about for years.

"Come on," he urged. "Give it one last shot. Nobody's around, you've got nothing to lose."

"OK, OK," I said, pulling a bathing suit out of my already packed trunk. "I'll meet you down there in five minutes." Looking back, I realized I had a premonition, a funny sensation in the pit of my stomach, as I picked up my towel and ran to the water.

The lake was empty when I got down there. I saw Greg, who was waterfront counselor, tying up the canoes. He waved when he saw me.

"You ready?" he yelled out. "I'll race you to the end of the dock."

"No fair," I answered, walking up to where he was working.

"Come on, Erika. Let me try to teach you one more time. You'll never be a good swimmer if you're afraid to swallow a little water. Just trust me." He demonstrated how to stretch out your arms and relax, then let your head go under, then bring it up to breathe.

"OK," I said, "here's to brain damage in action." I did exactly what he showed me and came up sputtering a few seconds later. "Forget it. You swim your way, I'll swim mine." I was amazed that I handled making a fool of myself in front of him so lightly. But he wasn't giving up on me just yet.

"Let's try it again," he said, putting his arm around my waist and letting his hands spread over my hips.

"The most important thing . . . ," I heard him saying, and all of a sudden I found it hard to concentrate. I was conscious only of his strong, hairy legs and how muscular his arms looked glistening in the late afternoon sun.

". . . is the breathing," he finished, giving me a look that told me he knew I had not heard a word.

"I'm breathing, I swear," I said, smiling. His head bent down, and we kissed in the water. First just our lips touched, then we kissed again. I was dizzy and held on to him tighter.

"We're only waist deep," he laughed. "I promise you won't drown . . ."

I closed my eyes, smiled, and buried my face in the pillow. It might've been January outside, but snuggled under the covers, I was drifting off to a warmer, happier place.

In the two weeks since the story broke, the media had been on a feeding frenzy. I hated coming home at three o'clock because the press people were constantly cruising past our house. Only by forcing myself to keep to a routine — tennis practice, *Melrose Place*, Dove-Bars — did I manage to keep sane.

What got me through, second, was the thought that I would be spending the weekend with my cousin Kathy. Kathy, a high-powered financial consultant, was twenty-eight, lived in Manhattan, and was engaged to the world's best boyfriend. She had black hair down to her waist and a body that was always mistaken for a dancer's. I'd always wanted an aunt, and Kathy didn't have any nieces, and we both felt that "second cousins" in no way near described our relationship, so Kathy asked her boyfriend (who was a lawyer) to draw up legal papers making her my "official aunt." The paper didn't mean anything in the outside world, but it was one of my prized possessions.

This weekend we were going to work on plans for her wedding. It was going to be incredible — Tavern on the Green in July, three hundred guests, an all-white bridal party with me as the junior maid of honor. Just like Kathy to be confident enough to know there'd be no mistaking anyone but her for the bride. I was even going to fly home from camp in Maine for that weekend.

I took the 9:45 train to Penn Station Saturday morning. Kathy was in the car waiting for me in our special designated spot across from Madison Square Garden. I was wearing my black cowboy boots, black jeans, a new cranberry silky blouse, and Matt's old authentic World War II leather jacket. Since our conversation I felt he owed me the right to borrow whatever he owned.

I opened the door, slid across the front seat, and kissed her. She smelled of Anaïs Anaïs. Her hair was pulled back in a high ponytail. Off-white shoe boots perfectly complemented her three-piece cream wool pantsuit.

"Hi, gorgeous. Nice blouse," she said. "How's it going?"

"You look like a bride already," I answered, ignoring her question. "What's on the agenda for today?"

"Well, I thought we'd go by Tavern on the Green first and go over the wedding menu. Make sure they go light on the duck pate and have enough chopped liver to keep Uncle Irving happy."

Sweet, quiet Uncle Irving was an accountant married to Aunt Belle. He—like most of the men in our family who were brave enough to stay married to one of the powerful, strong-willed Davis women—never complained about anything. "I'm not henpecked, just tolerant," he'd say when Aunt Belle kept him waiting with the car running for ten minutes till she said her final good-byes. He lit up when the Giants played good football, when the tax season was over, and when he ate chopped liver.

"Maybe we'll grab some lunch there, then go to Paperworks on Seventy-second Street to choose invitations. Then some window-shopping down Columbus Avenue before we meet Doug for dinner."

I couldn't have dreamed up a more perfect day. A warm sun and practically no wind made a lie of the freezing temperatures predicted by the weatherman. The store windows reflected crowds that usually walk double time almost sauntering, reveling in the gift of such a sparkling clear afternoon. Toddlers perched on their fathers' shoulders, the vendors who sold pretzels on the street corners took off their gloves, and even the hordes of yellow taxicabs seemed to be honking less belligerently. The lunch we "grabbed" in the Crystal Room—shrimp salad, iced tea, chocolate mousse—was wonderful. Michael Caine was there in a warm-up suit, dining on salmon in dill sauce. We chatted like girlfriends, giggling over the blue rinse the elderly women had on their hair, drooling over how cute our waiter was, and eating our desserts in teeny forkfuls, making them last forever.

"You have great taste, Erika," she observed as we walked out into the street after finalizing the invitation order. "I really appreciate your help."

"Are you kidding me?" I said. "Spending time with you is the highlight of my wretched life."

"Has it been majorly horrible?" she asked, slipping her hand through my arm. "I've been kind of selfish these days, assuming you'll tell me what's going on when you're ready."

"It's OK," I lied. "Dad's up and out by six-thirty every morning and doesn't come home till eleven. I hardly see him. Mom's trying so hard to keep it together that I feel guilty talking to her about anything much. She canceled our newspaper delivery, serves dinner at six o'clock, when the news is on TV, and closes her door a few minutes before eleven. So I don't bring it up. It's like I don't even have a brother . . . and school's school. Aren't you glad you asked?"

Kathy didn't say a word. We walked on in silence.

"Oh, Kathy," I moaned. "I can't lie to you. I hate my life. Can you believe what my dad did? I feel like the person I thought he was all these years was just an act. My real father would never risk his reputation for money."

"What does he say when you ask him?" Kathy held on a little tighter.

"That's the worst part. Nothing. He's so wrapped up in the business of hiding from us and making excuses and meeting with lawyers, he has no time to answer my questions. Besides, I wouldn't believe anything he says now anyway."

"And your mom?"

I thought for a second about treading lightly here, but the relief of being able to tell the truth to someone who cared about *me* was enormous.

"I know you think she's perfect," I began, feeling a little bad talking about my mom to her favorite niece, "but she's as annoying as Dad is."

Kathy waited.

"She cooks, she works, she cleans, she takes care of us . . . as if she were being filmed by *Candid Camera*. No one would ever know anything was bothering her. She asks about how I'm doing, never forgets to wish me good luck before a test, tells me we'll be OK . . . but it all sounds like she rehearsed. I wish she'd yell, or scream, or give me a hug that feels like there's a person behind it! She's like a robotic double of herself with the guts removed."

I was surprised Kathy didn't jump to defend her. She didn't say a word.

"So?" I said. "What do you think?"

"So?" she answered. "I think I don't envy you. I have nothing brilliant in the way of advice to give you—but I know just the purchase to help you hear less bad news. Come on. It's time to buy something completely ridiculous." Five minutes later we continued on, wearing our new teddy bear earmuffs.

That night we met Doug for Spanish food. I thought it'd be impossible for me to like whoever it was who would share Kathy's life, but Doug made it easy. He was handsome, funny, and it was obvious how much he loved her. Kathy and I compiled a list of our family's characteristics and habits so Doug would know not to laugh when he met them.

I started. "The way Uncle Sam follows fire engines whenever he hears a siren, regardless of where he's going."

"The way Cousin Florence has her hair

done like that woman in the B-52's—a red beehive."

"The way Uncle George and Cousin Jack sit so close to each other in the front seat of the car, there's enough room for another person."

"The way Aunt Molly wears knee-high stockings under her dress and then crosses her legs."

"How Great-Aunt Betty calls all of the young women in the family 'honey' and all the boys 'sonny' 'cause she doesn't remember anyone's name . . ."

I flashed for a second on how this geriatric crew must have reacted when they heard about my dad. I could hear them now, popping open their drug of choice—Valium or nitroglycerine—and burning up the telephone wires. Their comments would be interchangeable:

"What did I tell you? A man who tips almost twenty-five percent of a bill is spending money he didn't earn."

"Oy, the shame! Thank God his parents are dead so they don't have to see this."

"A beach house they needed? Like a hole in the head."

"I hope they don't ask me for money . . . The way you make your bed . . . that's the way you sleep."

"Whoa, whoa." Doug interrupted my thoughts. "I might have to rethink this decision of mine. Beehives, knee-highs, and memory loss aren't exactly recommendations for your gene pool, Kathy."

Kathy leaned over and gave him a long, soft kiss. "I'll just have to make the next forty years worth your while," she said, sounding just like Kathleen Turner. I made a mental note to ask her how she made her voice all low and throaty like that.

We got back to her apartment just before midnight. She put on *Saturday Night Live* and crawled into bed with me until it was over.

"I'm so glad you're my aunt," I said, kissing her good night. "Thanks for the best day."

"You're one of my favorite people, Erika." She paused. "Just promise me if you ever want to talk . . ."

"I promise," I said, drifting off into the best sleep I had had in weeks.

It rained all Sunday. We listened to music, read magazines, and talked. About 4:30 we finally got dressed, and Kathy drove me home. Traffic was murder on the Long Island Expressway—a normal forty-five-minute trip took almost an hour and a half. I didn't mind at all. Anything that would postpone my reentry into hell was fine with me.

It was dark when we pulled into the driveway. The house looked closed up, like no one was home. That's how we'd taken to living lately, quietly, in the shadows. The cars were in the garage, the curtains were shut tight, and the outside light over the front door timed to go on at 6:30 would be on soon. Kathy wasn't even going to come in to say hello. She was tired, she said, and had a big week ahead, but I was sure it had more to do with seeing my parents and not knowing what to say.

I gave her one last kiss and jumped out of the car, my overnight bag enriched by one pair of teddy bear earmuffs, one leftover chocolate croissant, a copy of the wedding menu, and two tapes Kathy had made for me of some new music she thought I'd like.

"You're the best," I yelled as she pulled away. I ran up the walkway and started rummaging through my pocketbook for the house key. Ordinarily I would've rung the doorbell, but these tense times made a ringing doorbell a cause for sweaty palms. All of a sudden the darkness was lit up by the popping of flashbulbs. I looked to my left and was blinded by the flashing lights.

Someone leaped out of the bushes and, talking very fast, said, "Hi, Erika, if I could just have a word with you. How do you feel about your father turning state's evidence, incriminating his boss, Raymond Schuman? He's your father's best friend, isn't he?"

My heart was beating double time. I couldn't find my keys. I put my finger on the doorbell and kept ringing and ringing. He knew my name. What was he saying about Uncle Ray?

"Go away. It's Sunday. Can't we have some privacy? Go away!" My voice was shaking.

"Did I scare you? I'm sorry."

I could make out that the picture taker was a short, skinny young guy in his twenties. He was wearing a dark ski jacket and jeans.

"If you're sorry, leave . . . Otherwise we'll call the police." My voice gained strength once I saw whom I was dealing with. My legs were still trembling, though.

Just then the door opened. My mother pulled me inside as if I were in the path of a speeding truck. She stared coldly at the young man outside.

In a tone I didn't recognize she said, "If you ever come near my daughter again, I'll break that camera over your head." Her voice was icy calm. The reporter backed away, apologizing and mumbling something about just doing his job. My mother slammed the door in his face.

We stood at the front door, and Mom held

me until my breathing returned to normal. I stood there, my head on her shoulder, for what seemed a long time. Then my eye caught a glimpse of my father at the top of the stairs.

"What did he say, Erika? Did he ask you any questions? Did you speak to him?"

Not "Were you frightened?" Or "Are you OK?" Or "I'm so sorry."

"He asked what I thought about you testifying against Uncle Ray. He knew my name and that Uncle Ray is your best friend."

"What did you say?"

"I said I'm calling the police as soon as I get inside. What could I say?"

"Good, good," my dad said distractedly. "You didn't tell them anything. That was good."

"No," I said, breaking away from my mother's arms. "It wasn't good, it was horrible." My voice sounded like someone was choking me. "Why didn't you come down if you saw that man bothering me?" I glared at him through angry tears. "You messed up. Why should I have to do your dirty work?"

I didn't get an answer.

"Doesn't my life until now count for anything? Can't you see I need your help now . . . ?" His voice trailed off.

"Well, I still need yours sometimes, too," I said, amazed at how cold I felt toward the man leaning on the banister. "Do you think you're the only one whose life is ruined? How come we have to protect you? You should be protecting us!"

My father looked away.

"Besides," I continued, "how could I tell anybody anything when you've never explained a word of what's going on to me?" All of a sudden I started to sob.

My mother moved closer and held me once again. This time I heard her heart beating even faster than mine. Her fingers felt freezing as she pushed back my bangs. There was no tenderness in this hug. It was as if by pressing me closer, she was managing to keep whatever was raging inside her in check.

It was all so horrible. I started thinking about Uncle Ray. If I felt betrayed and unprotected, how would he feel when he found out his best friend was testifying against him? I thought about the last time I saw him. He'd come with Dad to my last tennis match, not even six weeks ago.

I was having a tough time. The score was love–40, and gorgeous Gena Marshall of Greenwood High School was leading in the second set. Gena looked like she'd just stepped out of the beauty parlor. Her makeup was perfect, she wasn't perspiring, she was in full control of the match.

I'd lost the first set 6–1. Then I double-faulted, maybe three or four times. Totally demoralized I looked into the stands. My eyes met Uncle Ray's. His jaw shot out and he held up a clenched fist. I smiled. I relaxed enough in the second set to win in a tiebreaker, 7–5.

His words from the last time he watched me lose a match had replayed in my head. He'd looked like John Candy with frosty blue eyes. He wore a forest-green-and-pink warm-up suit that accentuated his 260 pounds. His voice had been a combination of tough and friendly—like Danny DeVito. "See that self-satisfied smile on that princess you're playing? Shove it right down her throat. You've got her number. Don't play her game. Play your own pressure game. Go on—belt her brains out with volleys!"

I played the rest of the match with his words echoing in my head. Ace. Fifteen–love. Ace. Thirty–love. I kept Gena on the offensive and won the game.

All of a sudden she was sweating more than I was. She was definitely tired. I glanced up to the stands once again. Now, when I'd expected a smile and a victory sign, Uncle Ray's eyes met mine, and he shook his head no—his way of telling me not to be cocky. Gena might be exhausted, but she wasn't beaten. I nodded that I understood.

Next, a perfect high lob. Then I forced a net play and won another point. I tossed the ball more to the right than usual, angling the racket sharply around the ball to give it a walloping spin. Another ace.

After the match we celebrated my victory at the diner. Uncle Ray took Dad and me out for ice-cream sodas. It was five-thirty, right before dinner, but with Uncle Ray you never concerned yourself with practical matters.

"Your poor opponent," he chuckled. "That glamour-girl-on-a-pedestal had her game broken before she knew what hit her."

"I remembered what you told me the last time I lost," I said giddily, still high from my come-from-behind victory, "about shoving the ball down her throat."

My dad winced. "Hey, hey," he said, "do you remember *my* words that clearly? Tennis is a game, after all."

Uncle Ray grabbed my hand across the table.

"You did great, Erika. Winners do what they gotta do to get the job done. You could've wimped out, turned into a jellyfish, after the first game. But you got guts. You got a strong spine." His eyes twitched. "Don't go too far away to college . . . I can't wait to watch *those* matches."

Now I stood on the staircase, with tears dripping down my nose. My mother reached in her pocket and gave me a tissue. She walked to the bottom of the steps and looked up at Dad.

Without any emotion she said, "I can't stay here hiding in this house anymore. I won't have Erika go through this ever again. We're moving out to my mother's tomorrow. There's room for you if you want to come."

And I had honestly believed things couldn't get worse.

CHAPTER 4

New York Herald Tribune

The longtime close friendship of Stephen Gresham and Raymond Schuman fueled an alleged web of corruption that turned the State Education Department into a racketeering enterprise. An executive of one collection agency has already told prosecutors that he paid Mr. Gresham $10,000 in bribes over 6 months on orders of Mr. Schuman.

IF I HAD FELT sorry for myself before, it was nothing to compare with now. I tried to make myself feel better by repeating in my head *Nobody's dying, we're not homeless, no one's being tortured.* But it didn't work.

I sat paralyzed on my bed, open duffel bag on the floor. My mother was yelling instructions, much louder than necessary, through my locked bedroom door. It was four o'clock on the dreary Monday following my weekend with Kathy and the encounter with the photographer.

"Just take clothes for the week and your books. Don't forget your toothbrush, your hairbrush, and that old flat pillow you can't fall asleep without. We'll come back in a few days for everything else. I've made the arrangements with Mr. Cannold to walk Bailey, no problem. It shouldn't take you more than ten minutes to pack. I'll be downstairs waiting."

All night I prayed that my dad would talk my mother out of moving. That he could convince her this would never happen again. But here she was giving me ten minutes to move out of the one space in the world I felt comfortable—my own room. Ten minutes. It took me that long to decide what sneakers to wear or whether to wear my hair up or down. Ten minutes. How did I know what I wanted to wear three days from now? What music I'd want to listen to tomorrow? And what about my telephone? What was I supposed to do—sit on Grandpa's lap when my friends called?

I dumped half my underwear drawer plus three pairs of sneakers into the huge duffel bag. Then I filled it to the top with jeans, sweatpants, sweaters, and sweatshirts. When I couldn't fit in another thing, I stuffed in my pillow. I dragged the bag down, bumping each step on the way. Mom was already sitting in the car. She took a look at the size of my bag, opened her mouth, and closed it again. Then she started the car.

"Let's go. Do you have all your books?"

"No," I said, throwing the duffel on the floor under the backseat and then slamming the front door as I sat down.

"What no? Why not?" She sounded annoyed. Her stuff was lying across the backseat, all neatly hung on hangers covered with plastic. There was one shopping bag with her shoes and toiletries and another with her phone book, her calendar, some magazines, and some makeup.

"I forgot the books."

"What are you, five years old? How hard is it to figure out you'll need your schoolbooks?"

I hated her at that moment. None of this was remotely my fault, but of course it was easier to yell at me than to face what she was really angry about.

"About as hard as it is to figure out how you came up with the idea that living with Gram is ever going to work out." I purposely sat there, daring her to go on.

"Look," she said, her knuckles tightening

around the steering wheel, "I have no time now to cajole you into a good mood. Sometimes you have to swallow your misgivings and just obey me." Her eyes stared straight ahead. "Now get upstairs and bring down the rest of your things." This last sentence was spit out between clenched teeth.

I opened the car door. "I'm not like you, Ma. I have no room inside to swallow any more misgivings. I'm trying hard not to cause you any grief, but I'm not going to pretend that I think this plan has a prayer of working out." I slammed the car door shut. "And I'm not a baby you can tickle and put in a good mood." I really resented her saying she could manipulate me that way. I'd do what she asked because I had no choice, not because she'd trick me into thinking this was going to be a pajama party.

"These are emergency measures, Erika," Mom said, trying to stay in control. She peered at the rearview mirror. "Please, just hurry and get your books. The reporters are bound to come by at dinnertime, when they expect Dad to be coming home. If we're gone—and they have no idea where—we have a shot at some privacy."

"For how long?" I asked sarcastically. "Till they ask Mr. Cannold?"

"He won't tell . . . because he doesn't know." She smiled grimly. "I told him I'll call every day to check in."

I ran out of the car, opened the front door with my key, and ran up to my room for my social studies textbook, my math workbook, and my chemistry Regents review book. I was back in the car in less than ninety seconds.

"Hopefully, this is only temporary, Erika," my mother said, her tone a little softer now. "Until this blows over. Maybe a month or so."

A month or so at Grandma's house was the equivalent of ten minutes to pack—off-the-wall. I'd never last. Even though my grandparents lived only nine blocks away, I knew I was about to enter a different land. A land where dust never survived long enough to hit the furniture. Where every meal had something green in it. Where life ended each day at 11:00 P.M. It wasn't only that Gram was the neatest person on earth (she ironed Grandpa's underwear and her handkerchiefs), she had this incredible list of things of major importance to her that meant less than nothing to me. Like making your bed and folding your bath towel. Like washing your hands before eating and never bringing food up to your bedroom. Like judging my friends by where in Florida their grandparents bought a condominium. I felt like running away. The pictures I'd seen of teenage run-aways living in Penn Station were the one thing that scared me more than my grandma.

Mom was quiet for a minute. I knew what she was trying to get straight in her head before she said it out loud. I saved her the trouble.

"Don't worry about me. I know that as much as Gram means well, she's going to drive me crazy. I'll just have to ignore the things she says that irritate me. You're my mom, not her."

"It won't be all bad, Erika," she said hesitantly. "You won't come home to an empty house after school. Your T-shirts will all be whiter than white and perfectly ironed. And you know, Grandpa's the best cuddler in the world."

"How does Gram feel about all this?" I asked, ignoring her efforts to placate me. "I mean, I know she's probably thrilled you're coming, but what about Dad?"

We were stopped at a red light. Mom sighed and thought for a moment. Then she said, "I can't lie to you, she's really upset. She keeps saying, if he needed the money, he should've come to her. I don't think she fully understands yet what's ahead."

Neither did I, but I didn't say that. Instead

I said, "She'll probably be extra sweet to him to his face and then curse him to Grandpa later."

"Probably," Mom agreed. "But you know how Gram feels about family. She might want to kill Dad for being so stupid, but she knows him since he's twenty . . . and she loves him very much."

"Then she'd better abuse him at least as much as she does me," I said, only half kidding, "because if she finds excuses for what he did and then throws a fit if I wear my jeans with holes in them, then I'm not going to survive this."

"We'll get through it," Mom said, as the traffic began to move. "As long as we're all together."

I wondered if Dad was included in her vision of togetherness.

I spent the rest of that night trying to cram what was in my duffel bag into the extra bedroom upstairs. It had been my grandmother's sewing room till that morning.

Grandma, with her frozen blond helmet of curls and her wardrobe of just-a-bit-too-tight rhinestoned and beaded warm-up suits (with sneakers to match), was a lot of woman for five feet one inch tall. She had this habit of talking to you in a voice loud enough to hear if you were fifty yards away—or in a coma— even if you were sitting right next to her. For as long as I remember, she'd always smelled of gardenias . . . a scent guaranteed to really open your eyes at the breakfast table. I never saw her without her hot pink lipstick, perfectly manicured nails, and a huge gold charm commemorating the dates Matt and I were born dangling from her neck.

"I made lots of room for you, dear," she'd said after dinner, proudly showing me what she'd done. "I just kept the bottom two drawers of the dresser."

The room had been the same for forty years. The wallpaper was a loud orange-and-green flowered print that might have been appropriate in a Brooklyn kitchen a few decades ago but was totally bizarre in a room where someone was supposed to sleep.

"It's a happy room, Erika," Gram said. "Sunny and bright. I always find it's hard to feel down in here."

I didn't think it would be hard at all.

"Where can I put my shoes?" I heard myself whining, but I didn't care.

"Under the windowsill?" Mom suggested,

really asking Gram's permission to leave them in plain sight rather than trying to satisfy me.

"Mmm. OK. Leave them out there for now. We'll see what we can figure out."

I looked around, trying to find a spot for my TV. It had been a present from Uncle Ray for my birthday. He hadn't called since that day in the car. I missed him. I knew I should be as upset with him as I was with my father, but I wasn't. Maybe it was because I was counting on him to find a way out.

I faked a yawn. "I gotta get started on my homework," I said, talking with my mouth wide open. "Then I'm going right to sleep. I'll see you guys in the morning."

My mom looked at her watch. It was seven o'clock, at least two hours earlier than I ever started my homework at home. She raised her eyebrows. "That's good. I'll wake you up at seven and drop you at school on my way to work."

That had always been my dad's job—to wake me and drive me to school. There wasn't an alarm clock loud enough to wake me on a school day. Dad used to wake me twice. First three raps on the door, followed by some cheesy greeting like "Once you get out of bed, the worst part of Monday is over" or "To-morrow's over-the-hump day, isn't this week just flying!" or "TGIF, TGIF. Hurry, you don't want to miss a minute of the best day of the week."

I'd grumble and say, "Two more minutes."

He'd go into the shower and come back five minutes later.

"OK. Now." Then I'd crawl out.

I wasn't sure how it would work with Mom. She and Dad were sleeping on the convertible couch in the living room. At least I hoped both of them would be sleeping there.

Except for forgetting my good hairspray and bringing the totally wrong clothes with me, the first few days really weren't that bad. I think it was the novelty of it. Dad did come to Gram's to sleep, but that was it. I knew he was there only by the way the bathroom smelled of Aramis, and because I saw his coffee cup in the sink.

I had to admit the suppers were great. No macaroni and cheese or pizza here. Instead there were lamb chops and meat loaf, mushroom and barley soup and mashed potatoes. As much as Gram read about modern nutrition, nothing could convince her that anything she cooked could possibly hurt you. How would we know she loved us if she served us puny beans and salads and smelly fish with bones? I gave my friends my temporary new phone number but asked them not to call unless it was really, really important. Otherwise I'd call them.

"Why can't I call you there?" asked Allison. "Your grandparents like me."

"It's not that," I replied. "The two phones in the house are in the kitchen and my grandmother's bedroom. She hears everything . . . even if she's not in the room. I'll call you when the coast is clear."

That was 50 percent of why I didn't want any calls. The other 50 percent was that I had no interest in small talk.

I used to live for hour-long conversations about nothing. But now I felt like the boy in the bubble in that TV movie: I heard and understood everything, I just couldn't get out to really be a part of things. The boy had no immunity to protect him from bacteria and viruses; I had no immunity to protect me from the attention of my friends. Whether they asked a million questions or they ignored the whole thing completely, I was miserable. It was easier being alone.

The bonus was being around Grandpa. This whole thing with Dad must've killed him, but no way would he ever show his disappointment to us. He was really tall for a man in his seventies, with thick, wavy gray hair, perfect teeth, and great posture. Always a news freak, he had been the first person on his block to get cable TV, just so he could watch the twenty-four-hour news channel. If Dad had committed a spicier crime, it might've been on *Court TV*, and in some perverted way Grandpa probably would've loved it. The best times with him were spent in silence: holding hands on a spring walk in the park, me sucking my thumb as he hugged me after an argument with Matt, and now, leaning on his shoulder, watching my father on TV.

I'd nestle in his arms after supper to watch the evening news. Mom and Gram talked in the kitchen, cleaning up the dishes, pretending none of what we were seeing was really happening. The TV was our primary source of information about what was going on with Dad. He rarely came home before eleven; he was spending his days and nights with Uncle Ray and their lawyers and government agents.

We never actually discussed what we saw, but I think we both felt better holding on to each other while we watched.

Sometimes Grandpa would say, "Geez, he's not a John Gotti, your father, but you wouldn't know it listening to this guy." Or "I wish I could talk to some of these people. Your father's not as smart as they're making him out to be." I knew he wasn't kidding. Even though it wasn't really a compliment, it made me feel better to know Grandpa didn't believe Dad thought up all the nasty stuff they said he did. Those half-hour stretches of time became the best part of staying at Gram's. Sometimes that's all you need—someone who knows how you feel, doesn't tell you it's wrong, and trusts you enough not to say a word.

Gram was the exact opposite. She never knew how I felt, always told me it was wrong, and didn't trust me enough to remember to flush when I went to the bathroom. I had never minded spending small doses of time with her; she taught me how to knit, how to tell if a cantaloupe was fresh, how to put my house keys between my fingers if I was ever alone walking at night. It was the everyday nitty-gritty that was tough with her. I think we both looked away a lot those first few days, but I knew it wouldn't last.

"Erika, dear," she chirped one morning as I was forcing myself to cram down the bowl of Total and half a banana she'd prepared for me rather than fight about the fact that I wasn't hungry in the morning and had no time. "What's that thing on your nose?"

Exactly what a person wants to hear first thing. "I give up, Gram, what's that thing on my nose?" I answered, in a tone I tried to make sound light and funny but came out (on Gram's scale) as rude and disrespectful.

"Don't be so touchy. Charlotte, you were never so touchy. I just wanted to offer some help on how to get rid of it, that's all. But if you like it there, I'll shut up."

Please God, I prayed. Just let me get through three more mouthfuls without exploding. She means well. She means well. But God must have been busy. "Gram, it's just a pimple," I said. "I get them all the time. They go away. I just don't like when people point them out to me, especially first thing in the morning."

From the corner of my eye I saw my mother put down her coffee cup. I could tell without looking what her face looked like. She'd be biting her lip, trying to think of how to change the subject before this grew any bigger. But it was too late.

"Oh, pardon me, I'm a people. Forgive me, I should have known. You're sixteen, you don't need a grandmother anymore. I should just keep my mouth closed."

"Ma, I don't think Erika wants you to keep your mouth closed," my mother weakly offered.

She was wrong. That was exactly what I wanted.

"One more thing, Erika, as long as we're

talking," continued Gram, gathering steam now. "I'd like you to be a bit more careful how you make your bed. It looks like a nine-year-old did it. It would take two more minutes more to do a beautiful job."

"OK," I said, pushing back my chair. "I gotta go or I'll be late."

"Sit down, young lady. This'll only take another minute."

"Can't it wait for later?" I said, pleadingly, looking at my mom. She was clearing the table and was no help at all, having resigned herself to the path of destruction ahead.

"No, later you'll be busy, too. Just a few things. There's no reason that a girl your age can't help out a little around the house. Your mother lets you get away with murder at home, but she's under a strain right now and I'm almost seventy-two. I'd like you to give me maybe two hours on a Saturday to vacuum, fold the laundry, change the sheets, things like that."

"Fine," I said, running to get my books. My heart was beating fast, and I knew my face was all red. Probably from holding in more angry words than a human body can contain. I knew this wasn't going to work out. Not having a place to invite my friends. Not able to have a private conversation. Forced to clean for my grandmother. And where was my father? How come he didn't hear any of this? He was busy with much more important things than my mental health.

We drove to school without saying a word. I was angry with my mom for not standing up for me, even though it wouldn't have done any good anyway. Grandma was relentless; no matter what you threw at her, she kept coming. Seventy-two, my eye. Gram could've lifted the car we were riding in on willpower alone.

The next day Mom brought over the mail from home. I hardly ever got any addressed to me, but I looked every day anyway, hoping there'd be something to surprise me. She handed me a few things.

There was my renewal bill from *Elle*, a brochure offering a course to raise my SAT scores by three hundred points, the J. Crew catalog, and a blue envelope addressed to me. It was printed very neatly, "Miss Erika Gresham," with the word "I" in parentheses before "Miss." I sat down in the kitchen with a glass of milk and three chocolate chip cookies. I didn't recognize the return address, but the postmark said Somerfield, Connecticut. I wanted the anticipation to last, so I took off my glasses and cleaned them with a napkin. Then I slowly opened the envelope, careful not to rip it. Inside was a card. There were no words on the front of the card, just an empty swing, all in watercolors, in the middle of a meadow in the summertime. Inside was printed "Miss you," all in flowers. On the inside of the cover was a short paragraph.

Hi Erika,

"What's *he* writing me about?" you might be saying to yourself. Well, I just heard from Scott what's been happening with your father. What a bummer. I figure you could probably use a friend who lives far enough away not to care about the gory details—but who's thinking about how you're doing. Anyway, it's been five months since camp and I thought maybe you'd like to join me in a countdown till we'll be complaining about flies, warm milk, bratty kids, and CITs not getting enough counselor privileges! You'd better be practicing your tennis, 'cause this is the summer I'm going to regain the manhood you destroyed last year on the courts.

Meanwhile hang in there. Remember sticks and stones and all that crap. And if you want to tell me how happy you were to hear from me, please don't hesitate. My return address is on the envelope.

Greg

P.S. Have you heard Luscious Jackson on DRE yet? They're awesome. I thought of you the first time I heard them.

I read the note over three times. A line of excitement made its way down from my pounding heart to deep inside my belly. Instead of thinking about how kind his words were, my mind kept racing back to my swimming lesson on the last day of camp. He had to remember, even if he didn't mention it. I ran my tongue along the inside of my lower lip, retracing the ridge that had been there from the pressure of Greg's kiss.

The next day after school I stopped at the stationery store. It took me almost a half hour to choose the right card to send back to him. I settled on one that was kind of lame but relatively harmless. It had a picture of Snoopy and Woodstock chatting in a sunny meadow. The words on the outside said, "Every once in a while it's nice to send a friendly hello to someone who's really special." When you opened it up, there was a huge "HELLO!" inside.

As soon as I got home, I made out the card.

Dear Greg,

You'll never know how good it felt hearing from you. I needed a reminder that there is a life to look forward to—and you always have a way of making me smile. The last six weeks have really been the pits. When we have a chance, I'll fill you in on all the dirt you've been lucky enough not to have heard so far. I'm living with my grandparents for a while, which is a major thrill in itself. That, along with hiding from nosy reporters (you wouldn't believe how rude those people are), feeling like a leper at school, and not knowing what's going to happen with my dad, makes this a tough time to get through.

But thanks to you, now I'm going to focus on five months from now. Yes, I'm coming back to camp. I can't let you ruin our chances of winning color war by writing the alma mater all by yourself. About the possibility of you beating me on the tennis courts . . . I admire a guy with confidence! Thanks again for thinking of me. Write again if you get a chance. I haven't had a pen pal since I was in fifth grade and we wrote to a class in Finland. I must've bored the kid I was assigned to. After just two letters, she never wrote back . . . See you soon.

Erika

P.S. I did hear Luscious Jackson. They're amazing. What do you think of Weezer?

I didn't read it over because I knew then I'd be whiting out half of it. What was the big deal? Just a note thanking a friend for his concern. All of a sudden after six summers I felt shy, like he was a stranger. Because he acted like a friend. Could life be more confusing? I put on a stamp and walked to the corner mailbox. He might not even write back. But I scared myself with how much I really hoped he would.

Three nights later the clock said 2:20 when I lay down to go to sleep. I turned to face the wall. Greg's note had the opposite effect of what I'd expected. The surge of excitement it ignited energized all my anxieties. Before, nothing that was happening in my life was important. I didn't care about my grades. My friends were boring. And the upcoming tennis championships aroused only dread because I knew I'd have to pretend they meant something to me.

I guess Greg's note had awakened that part of me that cared. And once I admitted that I cared about him, I started to care, actually worry, about everything I'd been trying to ignore. Now every problem flashed before me in terrifying Technicolor. Tonight even three aspirins didn't quiet my headache. Studying for my bio test was a total waste. I had always relied on my notes to get through Mr. Johnson's tests but, although I'd heard everything he'd said these past few weeks, I hadn't listened hard enough to understand a word. I'd made myself sit there and pretended to study for ninety minutes, but I couldn't tell you one concept that made sense.

The tournament to decide the division championship of the North Shore was just two and a half weeks away. I had been sleepwalking through practices lately, making shots from memory, like a policeman reading someone their rights. I knew Mr. DaMaio noticed, but he didn't say anything. You had to be hungry to win, and I felt like I was racing on diet pills. Instead of picturing victory, as Mr. DaMaio always encouraged us to do with imagery techniques, all I could visualize were the hundred and one ways I could embarrass myself.

In school that afternoon, lunch had been

a disaster. My good temper, which had been hanging by a thread, was beginning to fray. I found the babble about inserting tampons, the new wonder bra, and *90210* incredibly immature and annoying. Talk about my dad's crime had become old news in just a few weeks. It surprised me to realize that instead of being relieved, I felt even worse. I wanted them to know how tired I was from not sleeping, how nervous I was about what was going to happen, how much I missed my dad, how upset I was. But I didn't feel like talking about it. I knew I was being impossible and irrational, but I couldn't help it.

"So what's up with you?" Laura asked. It was the first time all lunch period a question was directed at me.

I shrugged my shoulders.

"I mean with your dad's predicament," she continued. "Anything going on?"

"His *predicament*?" I snapped. "Why don't you just call it 'a kettle of fish' like my grandmother does?"

"I'm sorry," Laura faltered. "What do you want me to call it?"

"Oh, I don't know. How about his 'undoing'? Or his 'tragic fall from grace'? Or his 'impending incarceration'?"

The table got very quiet.

"Maybe you should save some of that sharpness for your tennis game," Allison said.

"Maybe you should mind your own business," I hurled back, "even if you do get off talking about mine."

Allison bit her bottom lip. I could see that she was trying hard not to really let me have it.

"Look, Erika, you don't have a right to punish us for what's not our fault. Laura just asked you a question. You didn't have to bite her head off!"

I couldn't believe what I did next. I gave my best friend the finger.

"OK, OK, everybody calm down," Ingrid implored.

Luckily for all concerned the bell rang.

I shoved the wrappers from my lunch tray into my backpack so I wouldn't have to stop at the garbage can. Without turning back, I ran out of the cafeteria.

It was anticlimactic the next day when I got a 68, my first D, on my biology test. Mr. Johnson, my biology teacher, peered at me over his glasses when he handed me back my paper.

"I stay till five o'clock on Tuesdays and Thursdays," he offered kindly. "If you'd like some extra help . . ."

"Thanks," I said, staring down at my test

paper. I was afraid if I looked in his eyes, I would cry.

"This grade is not an accurate reflection of what you're capable of," Mr. Johnson continued. "I know things are difficult at home, but try to stay focused. I'll help in any way I can."

"I got an 86," announced Andrea, the girl who sat next to me. That really drove me nuts. Andrea, who thought you flattened out your breasts if you slept on your stomach. Andrea got an 86. Who cares? I thought to myself. Big deal if I got a bad report card. What could my father say—"Why, honey, is there something on your mind?"

"No way should you lose to this girl. Just use your head and play your own game." Mr. DaMaio was giving me his final words of encouragement. The final points that would decide the division championship were a few minutes away.

"Come on, Erika, give me the mantra," he enthused. "It's all up to you." I wished I cared just half as much as he did.

"Don't get mad and don't get scared," I repeated dully. "I will be relentless today. I will make this last game the best game of my life."

I couldn't have sounded less convincing.

This was the first important match I'd ever played that Dad wasn't coming to. It had been my choice. I'd told him I'd rather he not show up. I looked across the court at my opponent. There she was, Megan Daily, last year's division champ. Anyone who, after splitting the first two sets and tying 4—4 in the third set, didn't look even the least bit unnerved deserved not only to lose but to be demolished.

The match shouldn't have taken this long. I should have finished her off by now, 6—4, 6—2. I had her down by two service breaks, and now she was even again, but my concentration was gone. Instead of thinking about her strokes, I kept thinking about how, win or lose, Megan would go home to her own house tonight.

Stop it! I yelled at myself. Stop. Stop thinking.

Megan hit hard and crosscourt. I leaped, stretching my racquet, but the ball hit the upper part just below the frame and went into the net.

Where was the comfort I always got out of playing this game? I used to love the easy sweep of my arm as the racquet came into the ball, the little trampolining effect of the ball as it came off the sweet spot, the way, on the backhand, I could spin, then slice, each time sending the ball deep.

Today even the points I won didn't feel good.

"Stupid!" I yelled as I smashed the ball long. I had the whole court to hit. I could have dinked it over the net—she was way out of position. Instead I have to try and hit the line.

I glanced over to the stands. Mr. DaMaio had his hands folded in front of his chest and was pacing back and forth. He looked concerned, even though he was trying to appear calm and under control.

OK, I promised him silently, this one's for you. Miraculously I won that game, 5–4. Only one to go. I served hard to Megan's backhand, deep to the corner of the service box, and came in. Her return was chipped but low. I hit a forehand past her down the line. Yes! The score was 40–30 in my favor. I could win this sucker. I owed it to Mr. DaMaio and the rest of the team. One more point and it's the match.

I looked for Mr. DaMaio for one last dose of positive eye contact, and I couldn't believe it. There was Dad in baggy khaki pants and those sunglasses, watching me from the sidelines! If there was a place to duck or run, I would have. Why couldn't he have listened to me?

Megan waited for me to serve. How could I even hit the ball? I was shaky and unable to think about anything but how everyone in the stands must be whispering.

"Is there a problem?" questioned the official.

"No, I'm OK," I said.

My serve was hard and flat. Megan hit a great shot crosscourt, landing about four inches inside. I glanced over at my dad and met his eyes. Then I rubbed the dent mark the ball made on the clay with my foot.

"Wide," I called loudly, pointing outside the line. Megan had already started to pick up the ball again. Mr. DaMaio looked confused.

"Are you sure?" Megan yelled.

"Yeah, I'm sure." I smiled. The team was all cheering. Mr. DaMaio started clapping, too, first tentatively, then trusting me, much harder.

It was such a close call; it could've gone either way. I looked at my dad. He pretended he hadn't seen. But he did. I know he did, and he knew I knew he did. But we both pretended.

I quickly ran to the net to shake Megan's hand. It was only a matter of seconds before her dazed look would turn to anger. I knew if my gaze wavered, if my handshake was tentative, she'd notice immediately. I turned away from her face to run back to where the team was sitting.

"I admire your spunk, kid," said Mr. DaMaio, coming over to give me a hug. "I saw you were having problems with your concentration, but at the last minute you gathered your wits and you focused in. That's what makes winners."

Some winner, I thought. I'm the kind you told us to be on the lookout for, the one for whom winning is worth the price that lying and cheating extracts from self-worth. The one you said makes a joke of what competition is all about.

I searched for my father, wanting to watch his face as he heard what Mr. DaMaio thought made me a winner. He denied me that satisfaction. Without saying a word, he left the court and walked to the parking lot. I saw him get into his car and just sit there. I forced my attention back to the rest of the team. Everyone was hugging and smiling and congratulating me. As we made our way to the locker room, I noticed my dad still sitting behind the wheel, his head resting back on the seat, his eyes closed.

Pleasant thoughts, Dad, I silently communicated to him. Proud of me? The apple doesn't fall far from the tree and all that jazz.

I had just won two victories, and I never felt emptier in my life.

Rather than adding an extra three hours of Gram to my week, I decided what I needed was a wet kiss and cuddle from Bailey. I looked to make sure I still had the house key in my book-bag and then walked home. It felt a little strange not checking with Mom first, but, I mean, it was ridiculous having to get permission to go into your own house. I promised myself if I saw any strange cars parked outside, I'd just keep walking. As I got closer, the idea of lying on my bed for an hour or so, putting on some music, maybe making some hot choco-late, sounded exactly perfect. I could pick up some more socks and check the mail to see if I had heard from Greg yet. It had been three weeks, and I was beginning to lose hope.

I turned the corner and saw my father's car parked in the driveway. He was standing out-side, talking to two men who looked like they belonged to the beige minivan parked in front of Mr. Cannold's house. I noticed Mr. Cannold peeking out from behind the bay window in his living room. I put on the biggest, phoniest smile I could muster and waved right at him.

He waved back and then disappeared from sight.

"Gotcha," I chuckled to myself. Then I looked at what he was looking at. For a minute I didn't know whether to turn around and walk straight to Grandma's or continue on. It's my damn house, I thought; there's nothing wrong with going to say hi to my dog.

Dad looked startled when he saw me approach. He cleared his throat and then introduced me, "Tom, George, this is my daughter, Erika."

"Hi," I said, uncomfortable with how my dad's face turned red when he saw me glance into the open van. There inside, wrapped carefully in red quilted moving blankets, were my stereo, our VCR, and the twenty-five-inch TV my parents had had in their bedroom.

"I just came by to say hello to Bailey," I said, and quickly walked away from the three of them. The door was open, and Bailey went wild when she saw me. I sat down on the bottom step and held her tight while she wagged and panted and licked my face. There were no lights on, and the house looked sad and abandoned. I couldn't believe Dad had let those two strangers into my room. (He himself hadn't been in my room for almost a year since Mom made a rule that if I was going to keep my room looking that way, I had to keep the door closed all the time.)

I heard the storm door open. Dad walked in and sat down on the step next to me. Bailey looked up for a second, then looked away.

"I was going to tell you about this tonight, Erika. I didn't see any reason to let you know before it happened. But I wasn't hiding anything."

Did he want a medal? He probably had no room inside to hide one more thing. "So tell me now," I said sharply.

"The federal prosecutors insisted on confiscating those items. I explained that we'd had them for a long time, and they had nothing to do with . . . anything else, but they had a warrant."

"But that stereo was a present for me from Uncle Ray," I said.

Dad was silent.

I remembered that the VCR and the TV were also Uncle Ray-related. Dad had come home with both of them one day about eighteen months ago and told us he got a really great deal on them from a friend of Ray's. I couldn't believe this was happening.

"I'll replace them, Erika, I promise," Dad faltered.

When, I thought, after you come out of jail? Instead I took out my warning notice in math. "As long as you're here, you might as well sign this," I said, searching for a pen in my bag.

Dad looked at the piece of paper and said, "What's this about? You didn't mention you were having a problem."

"Like father, like daughter," I said. "Also, I'm not signing up for the tennis team next year." I couldn't believe I said that.

"Why not?" He stared right into my eyes.

I stared him down, daring him to say something about what happened at the tennis game.

"I don't feel like it. I have no energy lately. And I'm not in the mood to compete, you know what I mean?" If anything could get his attention, my quitting the team would do it. I knew I was making him feel bad, but I didn't want to stop. "It's like nothing is important enough to work up a sweat—not my grades, tennis—nothing."

"I really can't talk to you about any of this now," said my father in a shaky voice. "I have an appointment with my lawyer in half an hour."

"There's really nothing to talk about," I said. One part of me felt guilty for being so mean, but a larger part felt like being meaner still.

"Do you want a ride to Gram's?" he said, standing up wearily. "I can drop you on my way."

"Nah, I think I'll hang with Bailey for a while. I'll leave soon."

I watched from the front door as he walked to his car and got in. I noticed that his suit looked big on him and his hair was uncombed. He moved slowly, like he was walking through three feet of mud.

I closed the door so he couldn't see me watching. After he drove away, the house felt dark and creepy. I should've taken the ride but didn't want him to think I wanted to spend more time with him. I got up, went into the kitchen, and dialed Matt's number. I knew the odds were small that he'd be in, but it was worth a try. Mom had been calling him once a week since we moved, but I hadn't spoken to him since Christmastime.

"Hello," he answered, sounding preoccupied as he always did to anyone who had the nerve to barge in on his privacy.

"Hi, Matt, it's Erika. I'm so glad I caught you."

"Why, is anything wrong?" he said quickly.

"No, well—yes. Actually everything's been wrong since this whole thing started," I said.

"Living at Grandma's sucks, I'm doing lousy in school, I hate my friends, and you were right about Dad. He's a real lowlife."

"Poor baby."

I couldn't believe he said that.

"I wish you would call me, Matt. Aren't you curious about what's really going on? I know you're busy feeding the hungry, but I thought charity begins at home."

"It's been tough here, too, Erika. I have a statistics exam tomorrow that's a real killer. And Monday I have a biochem paper due that's got hours and hours of work left on it to finish."

"I know you're stressed, Matt. Nobody's as stressed as you." I took a deep breath and went on. "I go to school, too, you know. And I'm here and I have to deal with all this crap. I'm calling from the house now. You want to hear the worst? They just took away my stereo, our VCR, and the big TV. Two guys just came and took it."

"You want me to send you my box? I don't have much time to listen to it anyway."

"No, that's OK," I said, my heart sinking with the realization that he was trying, but he just didn't have it in him to give me what I needed. "Anyway, I should really be heading back to Gram. It'll be dark soon."

"Good idea, kid," Matt said, sounding relieved I wasn't going to ask for anything else. "Call anytime. I really want to hear from you. And if you change your mind about the stereo . . ."

"Thanks, Matt. Good luck on your test and your paper. When will you be home anyway? Isn't spring break next month?"

"Uh, yeah. But I'm not sure I'll be able to come home. There's an opportunity to work with this professor who's really amazing. The school has to pick two students to stay and help him with his research. I'll know next week."

"I'm sure they'll pick you," I said flatly. "Call and tell me when you find out."

"I will, Erika. Hang in there. Send my love to Mom and the old folks."

"Bye." I felt homeless and abandoned in my own kitchen.

CHAPTER 5

New York Daily Mirror

The scandal at the State Education Department has taken its toll, through public humiliation, lost esteem, and what several of those involved say is the widespread presumption of guilt. Mr. Gresham initially balked at cooperating but later pleaded guilty to racketeering and other charges. Scheduled to be a key prosecution witness in two corruption trials, he spends much of his time preparing to testify. He is expected to receive a substantial prison term.

I THINK I could've handled things easier if I'd had a better understanding of where my mother was at. Sometimes I'd overhear her talking to one of her friends, telling how furious she was with my father, calling him a son of a bitch, saying she had no use for him.

"He made a life decision that affected my

life, for the rest of my life, without me," I heard her say. "I don't know how I'm going to forgive him."

I wondered why she'd want to. There were loads of wives who left husbands for a lot less. Money was becoming a problem already, and I saw the strain and worry on her face. It irritated me how she kept her feelings under control, especially when Dad was around.

"I don't know how you do it, Ma," I said one morning as she drove me to school. "Don't you feel like running away from home?" I smiled inwardly thinking of the havoc that remark would play with her not-yet-fully-digested Wheaties.

She stiffened. "No, Erika, I don't." I could tell she was gathering her thoughts.

"You're right . . . Strangling Dad would be much more satisfying."

She clenched her teeth. "I think there's a little projection going on here, Erika. You're attributing to me the anger *you're* feeling." Could the woman annoy me more?

"No psychological lectures, Ma, please. I have no problem telling you or Dad that I feel what he did stinks. And I think he's a lowlife if he says one bad word about Uncle Ray. But I asked you first. If you say you're not thoroughly pissed at him I won't believe you."

My mother pulled the car over to the side of the road. She shut off the ignition and took off her sunglasses.

"I don't know where you come off talking to me in that tone!" she began. "How I feel about what your father did is for me to work out as best as I can. I'm sorry if you're disappointed that I'm not breaking dishes or throwing his clothes on the lawn."

Her voice got lower, but her words grew stronger. "I will not upset my parents any more than they already are." Then she finished me off with "And I wish to God that was a sensibility you inherited."

If she had said those words to me six months ago, they would've really hurt. But that morning they scarcely mattered one bit.

The next night, when I couldn't sleep, I came downstairs around midnight for a spoonful of peanut butter and a glass of milk. I saw my parents sitting at opposite ends of Gram's kitchen table discussing which bills to pay when.

"I'd take care of the auto insurance first," my father said. "We have a thirty-day grace period for the gas and electric."

"No, I'd rather pay the utilities and wait for a second notice from the insurance company. We've never been late before; I'll just say it was an oversight or we were away."

"Whatever you think, Charlotte," my dad said, knowing what a big thing paying debts on time was for her.

Since he was no longer drawing a salary, whatever money Mom earned plus a small sum they'd borrowed from Grandpa had to somehow be stretched and juggled to cover each month's financial obligations.

"I called the accountant about cashing in our bonds and your life insurance policy. He said he'd take care of it."

Dad nodded. "That should help us hang in there, at least through the end of the year."

They both sat up tall when they heard me; Dad looked embarrassed, Mom strained, from pretending there was nothing unusual about paying bills at this hour. I felt exiled to a chilly place far away from both of them.

I wondered, since Mom was such a stickler for doing "the right thing," how she could ever respect my father again. And I wondered if it was possible to love someone if you didn't respect them anymore.

Saturday Mom knocked at my door at nine-thirty and woke me.

"Want to go shopping?" she asked, standing in the doorway.

"Sure," I answered. "What do you have to get?"

She came into the bedroom, closed the door, and opened the window shades, letting in the gray light of February. For once I was grateful it wasn't sunny. Ordinarily I'd be annoyed if she opened the shades before I was fully awake, but I was glad she wanted to spend some time alone with me. Things had been strained between us since our blowup in the car, and if this was Mom's way of breaking the tension, I was more than ready to accept her unspoken apology.

"Next month is Gram and Grandpa's fiftieth wedding anniversary. I thought we could make them a little surprise party. You know, just the family and a few of their friends. I already have a freezerful of hors d'oeuvres at home that I made and never used for New Year's Eve, and we could do the rest of the cooking ourselves. I'll ask Grandma's sisters to bring the paper goods, soda, and desserts. What do you think? Today we could look for the invitations."

This was right up her alley—planning, organizing, inviting, and feeding. And I figured it was a perfect way to ease her conscience about the burden our stay might be inflicting on her parents.

"Great idea," I said, injecting a bit more enthusiasm than I actually felt. "It'll be nice, just the two of us, for a change."

My mother bent down and gave me a quick kiss. "I thought so, too. Take a shower and get dressed. We'll go out to the diner for breakfast."

We were ready to leave by ten-thirty.

"Where are you two off to in such a rush?" asked my grandmother. "I bought special bread from the bakery for French toast."

"Save it for tomorrow, Mom," said my mother. "Erika and I have a few errands to run."

"Such important errands that they can't wait till after you eat something?" Gram said, more than a little put out. "Where are you dragging your mother that's such an emergency?"

I wasn't surprised she blamed me for her disappointment over our missing breakfast. Nothing was ever Mom's fault. I never even heard her say that Dad was to blame for all that happened. She probably thought it was all my idea.

"Mom, Erika and I are going out for breakfast. She's not dragging me anywhere. I'm dragging her. The bread will be fine to use tomorrow. I swear, you make such a face when you don't get your way . . ." Mom grabbed my hand and pulled me out of the kitchen. "I'll try to explain to Erika that you really don't mean anything when you pick on her for no reason," she yelled as she slammed the front door.

I giggled as I ran down the steps. Mom was more aware of Gram's attitude than I thought.

"Thanks, Mom," I said. "Sometimes it's hard to figure what I did to make her think I'm such a rotten kid."

"She doesn't think that at all. It's just that she sees things as good or bad and anyone who doesn't do exactly as she says is bad. You have the guts to argue with her—I never did. She's not used to that. So she'd rather blame you than me—I'm a reflection of her perfect up-bringing, after all. Meanwhile, I'm proud of the way you stand your ground."

I savored the moment.

For the first time in weeks we were easy with each other. Breakfast was delicious, and we both ate like animals. Pancakes, sausage, home fries, buttered toast, and hot chocolate for me; bacon, two eggs up, home fries, toasted English muffin for Mom. I told her about

Greg's card and about my fight with Allison. Then I told her what happened when I saw Dad that day at our house.

"Did he tell you about the warning notice? Did he mention my quitting the tennis team?"

My mother shook her head.

"No," she said slowly. "He said you walked by the house when they came to repossess Uncle Ray's gifts. And you were upset. He was probably trying to spare me your warning notice. What subject are you having trouble in?" Her brow knit in a frown.

"You mean what subject am I having the most trouble? Math was the warning notice. But I think a few other teachers are just biding their time, giving me the benefit of the doubt." I tried to sound like it didn't bother me, but I know I didn't fool her.

"Is there anything I can help you with? Do you need a tutor? Should I go up to school and speak to your guidance counselor?" Poor Mom was looking alarmed.

"Take it easy, Ma," I said. "Everything hit the fan this quarter. There are two more tests before the marking period ends. I promise to try harder."

She nodded. "I know you will, dear. I'd be crazy to expect you to concentrate with the same single-mindedness as you did last semester. Just don't let your grades in your all-important junior year be another casualty of Dad's . . ."

She paused, searching for the right word.

"Stupidity?"

"Stupidity," she agreed. Then, without a breath, she went on to the next arena. "Now what's this about tennis? I think . . ."

"I know what you think, Ma," I interrupted. "I'm just not into it." I scanned her face and was satisfied she knew nothing about what had happened in the tournament. "Three years is enough. I'm not good enough to get into college on my tennis playing . . . and it's just not important right now."

"But how you feel now is not how you're going to feel in August," Mom protested.

"You think this will be better in August?" I retorted. "The way I figure, Dad should be going to jail right about then. There'd be nothing I'd like more than to play tennis in front of the whole school with everyone thinking about that instead of my serves."

Mom was so focused on her mission to keep me on the team that she completely ignored my reference to jail.

"I can't believe a girl who can stand up to my mother is going to give up something she loves because of dumb gossip. Promise me you won't say anything to Mr. DaMaio yet. Wait a while, OK?"

"OK," I said reluctantly, more because I was in no hurry to face Mr. DaMaio than because I agreed with her. Besides, she was on her best behavior. She had let the warning notice slip by, and I owed her one.

The diner was across the street from the Miracle Mile shopping center, which had the stationery store we were heading for.

"What do you say we leave the car parked here and walk off some of this breakfast?" Mom suggested.

I nodded and burped in reply. Mom made one of her what-did-I-ever-do-to-deserve-such-a-daughter faces, and we put on our coats. I noticed that she'd lost some weight and looked young and pretty. I wondered whether Dad saw the same thing when he looked at her. My mind flashed on her putting suntan lotion on his back, on hearing them lock their bedroom door. I shook my head to make the thoughts disappear.

We were standing at the cashier, waiting for change, when I saw Allison and her mom walk into the diner. There was no way we could avoid saying hello.

"Hi, Dale, you're looking great," Mom began, moving in to give her a kiss on the cheek.

Dale's eyes widened. "Charlotte, oh, you've been on my mind for weeks. I've been meaning to call. Allison told me you're at your mom's . . ."

They went on volleying appropriate social clichés back and forth.

Allison rolled her eyes and I smiled. We'd never talked about what had happened that day at lunch; I think we were both praying that it would just evaporate from our consciousness. We were still friends — just not the same kind.

"Any interesting mail?" she asked.

"No, nothing," I said sadly. "I mean, really, why should he write again? He told me he was sorry to hear what happened to my dad. I told him I appreciated his concern. It's a done deal. No biggie. I'll see him this summer."

"Sure. I believe that." She made a face. "Did you forget who you're talking to?"

"Almost," I said, suddenly serious. I felt miserable. "Look, about what happened at lunch . . ."

Allison put her hand over my mouth. "Save it, Erika. There's nothing to say. You were in bizarro world, and instead of going in to rescue you — I went in and joined you. The whole thing was due to how-they-say 'circumstances beyond our control.' Let's forget about it."

"I think you're wonderful to be out in

public like this." Allison's mom's voice broke into our conversation. She made some kind of clucking noise meant to be sympathetic as she kept shaking her head no.

Allison stood behind her, pretending to stick two fingers down her throat to mimic throwing up. Then she said, "God, Ma, she doesn't have beriberi . . . Why shouldn't she be in a diner?" I could tell she was embarrassed by her mom's clueless attempts to say the right thing.

"I didn't say she shouldn't," Dale said, giving Allison a we'll-deal-with-this-later-young-lady look. "I just meant . . ."

"I know what you meant," my mom said kindly, grabbing my hand to make our second getaway of the morning. "And I thank you for your good wishes."

"See you Monday," I yelled to Allison as my mom pulled me out the door. "And I thank you, too, for your good wishes."

The door was about to close just as Allison made believe she was getting something out of her eye with her middle finger. I laughed and gave her the thumbs-up sign just as the door slammed behind me.

That night mean-old-mister-middle-of-the-night made his third appearance in a week. Just like my school day was routinized—first period bio, second period gym, third period American history—so were my nights falling into a recurrent pattern. First I'd finish my homework about eleven o'clock and then try to study. I'd sit there, sometimes for over an hour, rereading the same pages, sometimes even reading them out loud to get my own attention. I took notes on what I read, then couldn't decipher them because my handwriting got so bad. About this time my headache would kick in. The pain felt like I was wearing ten too-tight rubber bands across my forehead, trying to restrain whatever's pounding to get out. Anticipating its arrival, I already have the aspirin handy and gulp down three with the same warm diet Coke I snuck up to the room after Gram went to sleep. After a while I get sleepy and make my first attempt to fall off to a land where I still slept in my own bed and won tennis matches without cheating. But instead of arriving at a destination of my choosing, I wind up hanging out in some *Twilight Zone* vision of the future. In my favorite I'm in a boxing ring. I'm fighting for what seems like hours. I'm mean and strong, and every opponent is defeated. But they keep coming. They're all wearing hoods, so I don't see their faces. They don't know I have weights in my gloves, and I knock them all out. I'm starting to get tired. My hands are so heavy I can barely lift them. I ask the referee how many more rounds I have to fight, but he doesn't hear me. Nobody can. Only I can hear myself speak. "This is a mistake," I scream. "I don't want to do this anymore. Let me take off my gloves, and I'll show you why I keep winning. Please let me lose. Knock me out." But there's no relief. I keep punching and ducking and jabbing and silently crying . . . till I wake up, unbearably guilty, thoroughly exhausted.

A few nights later was a slow news night for Grandpa and me. Just some minor stuff about lawyers fighting back and forth and the judge threatening one of them with contempt if he didn't stop talking to the press so much. They interviewed Uncle Ray as he was walking up the steps to the courthouse. Even though it was cold and windy, he looked like he was sweating. He had dark circles under his eyes, and he needed a shave.

"These trumped-up charges are garbage," Uncle Ray said. "This is New York politics at its worst. I am confident that when all the evidence is brought forward for the judge to examine, he will find me innocent on all charges."

Grandpa and I looked at each other.

We were both thinking the same thing. How come he didn't say "find *us* innocent of all charges"?

"Erika," my mom called out from the kitchen, "phone for you."

"Who is it?" I yelled back, too comfortable in Grandpa's arms to move. "If it's Allison, tell her I'll call her back."

"It's not Allison," Mom said. "It's Gregory, a friend of yours from camp."

I sat up so quickly I almost broke Grandpa's jaw. He smiled and said, "Gregory must be an important friend to get you to move so fast— or at least a handsome one."

I stood up. "He's very nice. He wrote me last month when he heard about Dad, and I wrote back to him. He lives in Connect-icut."

"Well, go then, it's long distance," Grandpa said, taking a swipe at my behind with his newspaper and missing.

I ran into the kitchen, where Mom and Gram were having a cup of tea. There was no way I could talk to Greg in front of them.

"Gram, this is kind of personal. Could I use the phone in your bedroom?"

Thank God she was in a good mood. "Sure, *mein kin*. You can close the door if you want.

All I ask is that you just take off your shoes if you lie on the bedspread."

"Thanks."

I heard her ask Mom as I ran out of the room, "Who is this Gregory who makes her cheeks so flushed?"

"A nice friend from camp, Ma. I'm sure if it's important Erika will tell me later."

I slammed the bedroom door shut and dove on the bed. I caught my breath and then picked up the phone.

"I have it," I called sweetly, not sure, if Gram was holding the receiver, how soon she'd put it back on the hook.

The phone clicked. "Hello, Greg?" I said.

"Erika, hi. What's up?"

I hated "What's up?" What are you supposed to say? I came up with a scintillating "Nothing much, what's up with you?" I just had to put the ball in his court for a minute to get my head together.

"Nothing too much. I was thinking about you and didn't feel like waiting till you got my letter and then sent one back before finding out how you were doing. Besides, I think I'm too much of a nineties kind of guy to keep writing. Unless we faxed messages back and forth. That might be unique."

I laughed. "That sort of defeats the purpose, but, hey, I can't be too particular. I've been kind of low in the support department, so you name the method and I'll communicate your way."

It was quiet for a moment. Then he quietly said, "Is it really that bad? I've been reading a little about your father in the newspaper. It's so slimy how your life becomes everyone else's business."

I pictured his face. He always had this intense look when he was concentrating. Even if he was just trying to figure out the lyrics of a song, his forehead wrinkled up like he was responsible for solving the problems of the world.

"It's slimy, all right," I said. "It wouldn't be so bad if people talked about it in front of me— but they don't. I guess they're embarrassed or afraid they'll hurt my feelings. But the minute I walk away, I know that's all they talk about."

"Listen, I know it's easy for me, but being far away lets me see things a little clearer. Whatever they're saying, they're saying about your father, not you. I know it hurts when people talk about someone you love, but *you* didn't do anything wrong. He screwed up. They're talking about *him*. Anyway, what bad thing could they possibly say about you—that you're loyal to your dad?"

It was wonderful hearing how worried he

sounded. Even if he mistakenly thought that what other people were saying was the worst part. No way could I tell him that love and loyalty were not what I felt for my dad. It was hard enough admitting that to myself. I definitely wasn't ready to share such ugly thoughts with Greg.

"Thanks, Greg. I forgot how easy it is to talk to you. But I'm tired of my sad story. Tell me about you."

We talked for almost half an hour. He told me about being up for captain of the soccer team, about how upset he was after getting a C in physics, about a fight he had with his mother over how he spent the money he earned from his after-school job.

Suddenly I remembered this was a long-distance call. "Greg, I think we'd better get off the phone. This is costing a fortune."

"Don't worry, Erika. I pay my own phone bill. And if I lived closer, we'd probably be spending time together and it'd cost me more," he laughed. "But I have to admit, I am feeling a little guilty."

"About what?" My stomach tightened. Here it comes. He has a girlfriend.

"I'm sorry about your father, but if it hadn't happened, I probably wouldn't have found a good enough reason to call you. You've been on my mind a lot since last summer. But it's awkward calling just to say hi. His trouble gave me an excuse."

"Oh," I said, hoping the relief in my voice didn't sound as obvious to him as it felt to me. "Well, then, maybe I'll have to work on hating my dad a little less for what he did."

I could tell that was the perfect thing to say.

"OK, then. Remember, if anyone bothers you, tell 'em you know a guy in Connecticut who thinks they better back off if they know what's good for them."

"OK, I will." By now I was lying on my back with my eyes closed, trying to memorize what his voice sounded like so I could replay it in my mind till I heard it again.

"I'll speak to you soon."

"Bye." I hung up the receiver and just stared at the ceiling. About fifteen minutes went by, and there was a knock at the door.

"Erika, are you OK?" Gram asked anxiously.

"I'm fine," I said dreamily.

"Can I come in? I just want to put down the laundry."

"Sure, it's a free country," I said, seeing my sneakers on my feet at the same time as Gram did when she opened the door.

CHAPTER 6

New York Gazette, *Editorial*

Sources close to the investigation announced today they would ask the grand jury to indict Stephen Gresham unless he agrees to cooperate more fully in their investigation. This public prediction of a criminal charge unless a witness cooperates is new—and worrisome. Bribery and racketeering must be dealt with, but not in a way that threatens our liberties.

A PHRASE that haunted me, that I heard almost every day on TV, was "messages left at the Gresham house on Long Island brought no return calls." It's one of those sentences you hear when the press tries to convince you they're trying to bring you both sides but one side just won't cooperate. The truth was they really didn't care about what we had to say. There'd be no surprises, no spicy revelations from the

Greshams. The press knew we were all forbidden by Dad's attorneys to say anything about the case. They also knew we hadn't lived at home for weeks. If they could find Roseanne in Italy and JFK Jr. on some tropical island, they could've found us nine blocks away if they'd wanted to. Silently I planned what I would say if I could call them back.

"Hi, this is Erika Gresham, daughter of Stephen. I hear you want to ask some questions . . . I'll answer yours if you answer mine. I'll go first. What gives you the right to camp outside my door twenty-four hours a day, scaring my family so much that we have to move out of our home? Where is it written that it's OK to hide in the bushes, follow my mom to work, and ask our neighbors what kind of people we are? If what you want is the facts, why aren't you talking to the lawyers? We know less than you do, so get out of our faces! I read recently about a guy who was convicted of murdering his parents. You said he showed no remorse, admitted no guilt, and had a depraved indifference to human life. That describes you guys perfectly." I'd slam down the phone.

I felt much wiser than my silly friends, who still believed that newspapers printed only the truth. I thought it unfit to publish that we were "in seclusion" (one block off busy Northern

Boulevard is scarcely the middle of the woods) or that the money my dad took was spent on things he never bought. I thought it wrong to print details about weight my dad lost when he went to a spa last spring (what did that have to do with the price of beans, as my Uncle Irving would say). And even though the truth was that he *had* taken kickbacks, I thought it was very wrong for the press to portray him as evil before he was tried, much less convicted, of any crime.

I could tell that Mr. Datz was closely following the story. You would think a man teaching American history would sympathize with one of his student's families being treated so shabbily in the name of freedom of the press, but he acted like he took it personally that my grades had gone down.

"No one who got less than an eighty on this test has a prayer of passing the final," he said one morning, looking right at me and the 73 he'd placed on my desk. "I don't know, people, how you expect to get by in this world without thinking. I give you the facts; it's your job to make the connections. I don't believe in spoon-feeding high school juniors."

"You don't believe in teaching them either," I muttered. It was hard for me to write essays about truth, justice, and fairness when I saw firsthand it was all a joke.

"Excuse me, Erika, is there something you wanted to say?" he demanded, standing behind his chair with both palms pressed on his desk.

I'd given him an excuse, and now he was out to get me. I waited to be humiliated in front of the class.

"I just don't think you realize how much material the test covered," I said. "It was on five long chapters, and we only had two days' notice. If you had . . ."

"Oh, is that what you said?" he interrupted. "Funny, it didn't sound like that to me. Jeremy, what'd it sound like to you?"

Jeremy was a short, quiet, A-plus student who sat in front of me. He never really made eye contact with anyone, never took books home to study, and never raised his hand in class.

"I didn't hear her," he said softly.

"What? Speak up," Mr. Datz said loudly.

"He said he didn't hear her," said Scott, who sat next to me.

I turned to him and smiled gratefully.

"What are you, his microphone?" Mr. Datz said, his fury growing. "If you were as good at hearing me as you are at hearing him, you wouldn't be in danger of getting a D in this class."

"Just trying to help," said Scott, winking at me, not at all disturbed by Mr. Datz's anger.

Mr. Datz knew he'd never crack Scott. He returned to me with renewed venom.

"You know there's more to getting into college than playing tennis," he said, glowering. "Your junior year grades are crucial . . . I can't believe you've become so lax."

Now it was my turn to be furious. "I am not counting on tennis to get me into college, Mr. Datz. It's just very hard for me to memorize proclamations, amendments, and laws that sound so perfect on paper but don't work in the real world."

"Like what?" came a voice from the back of the room. It was Stacey, always tan, always tawny Stacey, who'd had it in for me ever since I had taken her place as highest-scoring player on the tennis team. She was a combination of Tori Spelling's looks and Shannen Dougherty's personality—the worst of both worlds in zip code 11507.

"Like respecting people's privacy and treating them as if they are innocent until proven guilty in a trial. Like not coloring facts to fit into an already predetermined point of view. Like not looking through a family's garbage to

126

find out they bought raspberries and using that to prove they're wealthy and spend money carelessly." I could tell my face was all red.

"So you're saying your father is honest, and everybody's picking on him for no reason?" Stacey countered. She shook her head and rolled her eyes. "Come on, Erika, I'm not saying your father's a bad guy, but it's hard to believe he had nothing to do with this whole disaster."

The class was quieter than I ever remembered.

Mr. Datz leaned back in his chair with a self-satisfied grin. He was enjoying himself.

"I didn't say he was innocent," I said through gritted teeth. "And I didn't say he was guilty. But what you just said is exactly what I'm talking about. You should major in journalism. You'd be great on *Hard Copy*."

"Don't be so defensive," Stacey said patronizingly. "You're so thin-skinned! I wasn't attacking you. I just think where there's smoke, there's fire . . . and so does the *New York Herald Tribune*."

"This is a white-collar government corruption case, not a kidnapping," I finished lamely. "It's not sexy and there's no surprise endings, so the media is trying to spice up whatever boring evidence they uncover with personal trivia. Whether my dad's guilty or not, it's no one's business how much money he owes on his Visa card or where he and his friends like to eat dinner. How could it possibly be relevant that Raymond Schuman likes to drive sports cars or my dad's business went bankrupt years ago?"

"The public is just curious. They want to be entertained by someone whose problems today are worse than theirs," Scott said, half sitting in, half lying across his chair. "Don't sweat it, Erika. They'll forget you the day after they stop covering the story."

"That's not good enough, Scott, because *we'll* remember it always."

The bell rang. Everyone gathered up their books and left for their next class. I knew by lunchtime the whole cafeteria would know every word Stacey and I had exchanged, plus a few we hadn't. As I left the room, I saw Mr. Datz talking to Stacey.

"I'm sorry if I came on too strong," I heard her say.

"Don't apologize," Mr. Datz reassured her. "It was one of the best exchanges we had all semester."

Disgusting.

That Saturday night was my grandparents' fiftieth anniversary party. Matt really tried to make it, but between his project, finals, and how expensive the airfare was to come in for the weekend, he just couldn't swing it. I was glad in a way. The tension of keeping a secret from Gram, mixed with worrying about how Dad would do facing the whole family for the first time, was enough for me to think about. I couldn't handle a confrontation with Matt. We got Gram and Grandpa out of the house by buying them tickets to the Saturday matinee performance of *Phantom of the Opera*. It was also the only way Mom could be sure they'd stay away long enough to set everything up.

The invitation said 6:30, but Gram's whole side of the family, along with being loud, had the ridiculous habit of showing up early. By 6:20 there were forty people standing about. Just like in high school, everyone broke up into cliques. There were the bridge game partners stationed by the vegetables and dip, Grandpa's golf buddies standing close to where the hors d'oeuvres came out of the oven, the brothers-in-law (Grandma's sisters' husbands) in the backyard stealing a smoke behind their wives' backs, and, of course, the sisters, whose normal conversation drowned out the soft background music Mom put on.

"She's gonna die," said Rose, refolding the

napkins Mom and I had so carefully arranged on the dining room table.

"I know just what she's gonna say when she walks in," said Molly, putting toothpicks in the tiny knishes. "She's gonna say, 'Son of a gun, you really pulled it off.' Cleo would bet any amount of money that no one could ever put something like this over on her."

"You're wrong," said the last sister, Shirley, who was Kathy's mother. "She's gonna say, 'I knew something was going on, but I didn't want to spoil the surprise.'"

"Do you think she knows?" asked Rose.

"No," said Shirley. "She just won't give anyone the satisfaction of thinking they got the upper hand. She's crazy like that. She can't admit there's anyone alive smarter than her."

The three sisters all chuckled. It was amazing that no matter how much they loved and trusted one another, each would say the worst things about her sisters, both face to face and behind their backs. But let someone else say anything negative or even just agree with them, and they'd lynch you. Lucky for my dad that they always liked him.

"You look like you lost a few pounds, Stephen; that's good," Aunt Rose said to my father as she greeted him.

"Every cloud has a silver lining," my dad

replied. His lips were smiling but his eyes weren't.

"If they gave to the subways and the parks the same attention they're giving to you, New York would be a lot safer," Aunt Molly griped. "I'd like to see the tax returns of all those lily-white prosecutors."

"It's not their fault," my father said awkwardly. "They're just doing their job."

"Like Nazis." This from Aunt Shirley. "No matter what happened, Stephen," she continued, "you don't deserve this." She touched his face. "Of all the people," she said softly, "I would never wish this on—you would be one."

"I'll be OK," he answered with more conviction than I was sure he felt. "It's Charlotte and Erika I worry about."

I pretended I didn't hear.

Not everybody was quite so kind. There were lots of conversations that just stopped cold as I passed by. Some people just lowered their voices to loud whispers. And some couldn't care less who heard what they had to say.

"He never fooled me, never," trumpeted cousin Morty, a conductor for the Long Island Railroad. "When his business went bad, I told Selma he pulled out plenty before going under. Did you hear he went to a spa last year? A man goes to a spa? You got too much money when you start doing weird things like that."

"It's not the money that bothered me," answered his brother Charlie. "It's the way he would call, like a big shot last minute, and say, 'I just got my hands on two box seats to the Mets, you want 'em?' Like I couldn't afford tickets to a baseball game if I wanted to go."

"And that big fat friend of his," sniffed Selma, Morty's wife, not to be one-upped. "The two of them together look like those wrestlers from Japan. Something's funny, if you ask me, between two grown men who work together, vacation together, get into trouble together. You know what I mean? It's unnatural for a man to have a friend like that."

Her sister Rhoda rolled her eyes. "I don't want to start rumors," she chimed in, leaning into the circle where the four of them were standing, "but I heard Stephen's father once had a girlfriend. In the forties. In Brooklyn. I forgot who told me now, but what's the difference? If you grow up in a house like that, what are the odds you're going to grow up without getting into trouble?"

That shut them all up for a minute. It was all too ridiculous for me to get upset about. Even if I confronted every story, by the time I was done they'd manufacture four more. God bless families.

My job was to stand near the door, hang up coats, and direct the guests to Dad, who was tending bar. Mom gave him that job to give him something to do. She was all over the place, checking off things on her list (6:05 put franks in the oven, 6:20 unwrap bread, 6:40 take out coleslaw and potato salad), mingling and glancing nervously out the window.

The doorbell rang, and Kathy and Doug came in. My mood improved immediately.

"How's it going?" Doug asked, bending down to give me a kiss.

Kathy handed me a long, black, fur-lined leather trench coat that smelled as good as it felt. "Can I see you for a minute?" she whispered.

"Sure, follow me," I said. When we got upstairs, she shut the door behind her.

"Don't be upset," she said, fidgeting with my ponytail, "but there's a car down the block with a guy in it who's taking pictures of everyone as they walk in."

"Pictures of this crew? The press is taking pictures of this crew?" I started to laugh. "Who do they think is coming? O. J. Simpson? What a waste of time!"

133

I couldn't believe that the newspapers finally found us and, tonight of all nights, were camped outside Gram's house!

"The best revenge is to let that creep freeze to death out there waiting for the pope or whoever he's waiting for," I said, carefully placing Kathy's coat on the best spot on the bed.

"Seeing him really threw me," Kathy said, giving me a hug. "But you're right, the best thing to do is just ignore him."

"No," I said suddenly. "The best thing we can do is let him know we know he's here making a fool of himself. Why should he think he's cool enough to have done his job without us spotting him? Will you take my place at the door?"

I ran downstairs and put together a plate of franks in a basket, some chopped liver on tiny rye bread, and a few potato knishes. I covered the plate with tinfoil and ran out the back door. I went up to the black Chevrolet parked a few doors down the block. There was one guy sitting in the driver's seat. He pretended to be reading the newspaper when he saw me walk toward him. I knocked on his window.

He got flustered and tried to open the window but couldn't without turning on the car. He opened up the door instead.

"Yes? Can I help you?" he said, doing a poor imitation of an innocent bystander.

"No, not really. I just figured it might be a few more hours till President Clinton gets here, and you might get hungry. This is just a little something to keep your stomach from talking."

He took the plate from me without saying a word.

"Oh, and by the way, my grandparents are expected in about ten minutes, and my grandmother has eyes in the back of her head. If you take a picture and she figures out who you are and if that upsets her right before she goes in to be surprised for the first time of her life at her fiftieth wedding anniversary party, I'll be back, and I promise I will ruin your evening."

He just stared with his mouth slightly open.

I ran back in the house without turning around.

I looked over at Dad at the bar. He was trying hard to appear natural and was laughing with Kathy's father, Uncle Frank. I noticed how thin and pale Uncle Frank looked all of a sudden. I knew he had a lot of business headaches, but I hated to see him looking so tired. He had his arm around my father and was whispering some joke in his ear.

"Your dad looks like he could use a vacation," I said to Kathy.

"Funny, I was thinking the same thing about yours," she said.

Kathy went to get Doug something to eat, and I just stood there staring at my father. At that moment I caught him pretending to ignore two of Gram's friends who were making a big show of pretending to ignore him. I felt sorry for him the way I would for someone in a TV movie. Only there he'd be punished and forgiven by 11:00 P.M. I don't think the two of us exchanged fifty words all week; "How's school?" "Fine," I'd lie. "How'd your day go?" "Pretty good," he'd lie. I think we were both grateful nothing more was expected. I stopped kissing him good night right after that last car ride to Edgemont. The thought of touching him made my stomach churn. At least he had the good sense to stay away.

I must have stood there for a while. I was startled when Uncle Frank came over with two plastic cups. He had his usual vodka and tonic in one hand and a Coke in the other. He offered me the Coke, and I took it eagerly.

"I didn't even know how thirsty I was. How did you know?" I said, giving his hand an appreciative squeeze.

"Us quiet guys know a lot of things the

women in this family don't give us credit for," he said with a smile. "If you won't think I'm butting in, I'd like to share something with you that's been on my mind."

"Sure, Uncle Frank, what is it?"

"Sometimes we think because we love someone, we know all there is to know about them. And why they do what they do. And lots of times we don't."

I felt my face flush. I wondered if Dad had said anything to him about me. As if he read my mind, Uncle Frank said, "I may be way off base here, but I think if I were you I'd feel like I was mowed down by a runaway train. I'd be too angry to care whether the motorman was drunk or fell asleep or was distracted or misjudged his speed. All I'd be feeling is hurt. And all I'd be thinking is that he's to blame for my pain."

I listened quietly.

"But maybe his brakes failed. Or the track was slippery. Or the dispatcher made a routing error. Maybe the motorman wasn't completely at fault."

"If that were true, why wouldn't he tell me? Shouldn't he apologize even if he wasn't one hundred percent to blame? And what if he acted like he didn't even notice he ran me over?" My hands were ice-cold.

"I don't know the answers to your questions, Erika," Uncle Frank confessed. "All I'm suggesting is that maybe you don't either."

"He's the parent, I'm the child. I shouldn't have to do all the work."

"No, you shouldn't," he agreed sadly. The sympathy in his eyes was so sincere I had to look away.

"You know, I think the reason I love Kathy so much is because she's your daughter," I said, giving him a kiss on the cheek.

"Well, it's nice that someone acknowledges I had something to do with raising her." He laughed.

The party was a huge success. Grandma surprised all of us and just cried and cried when she came in. Grandpa was happy but I think a little embarrassed over the fuss. They got theater tickets, three picture frames, and only one totally useless silver tray. Several couples chipped in to send them to the mountains for a four-day weekend in May. And Kathy, outrageous to the end, bought them satin sheets.

"They're very sexy," she said to Gram as she opened the box.

"What makes you think we need satin sheets to feel sexy?" Gram answered, leaning over to give Grandpa a kiss.

I searched around, looking for Mom, to make sure she'd caught it. I saw her in the corner. She was looking at Dad straightening up the other side of the room. I was glad she hadn't missed such a sweet moment, till I noticed that her eyes were filled with tears.

CHAPTER 7

New York Tribune

Federal prosecutors have worked out a deal where Stephen Gresham will testify against other state officials and be allowed to plead guilty to reduced charges of racketeering. His testimony is expected to implicate many old cronies, including his best friend, Raymond Schuman. At stake will be not only the liberty and financial futures of the defendants, but also the credibility of the government's anticorruption effort, which has so far had more exposure in the news media than in the courtroom.

WE FOUND OUT Uncle Frank was dying about two weeks after the anniversary party.

"He thinks he's a Christian Scientist," said Grandma after we heard the news. "He never once went to a doctor in twenty years. He's the only one in the family who doesn't know his cholesterol level. And my sister, she's like a camel with her head in the sand, she doesn't see what's right in front of her."

"Come on, Cleo," said Grandpa. "Frank's always been in great shape. He never went to the doctor because he never had a complaint. Why, do you think if he went for checkups this wouldn't have happened? You think cancer's a punishment for not getting a physical every year?"

"Oh, Willard, I'm not saying that. But maybe they would've caught it before it spread. Maybe at an earlier stage there'd be something they could have done." Never did being right bring her less satisfaction. With all the angry words let out of her, she suddenly looked very tired.

We were sitting around the living room late Sunday afternoon. Kathy had called Saturday and told Mom the news. Grandma and Grandpa went right over to Uncle Frank's house and spent the rest of the day. They were telling Mom, Dad, and me what they had learned.

"Does anything hurt him?" I asked, hoping they would lie to me if the answer was yes.

"No," said Grandpa. "Any discomfort he

141

might feel is taken care of with medication. Except for feeling exhausted and not being particularly hungry, he feels fine."

"How's Aunt Shirley?" Mom asked.

"You know my sister," said Grandma. "She talks about it like it's happening to someone else. I think she's still in shock."

"Do they say how long?" said my dad quietly. He was staring out the window and pulling absentmindedly at his mustache. I got a chill from the verbal shorthand he used to ask his question.

"Not long," Gram and Grandpa answered at the same time.

"It's too far gone to do any surgery, and the doctors feel that he's too weak to tolerate strong doses of chemotherapy," explained Grandpa. "But his spirits are wonderful, and if there was ever a man to deserve a miracle . . ."

We just sat there, nodding our heads as we silently finished his thought.

"What about Kathy's wedding?" I questioned, breaking the silence. The minute the words were out of my mouth, I felt selfish for even asking.

"I spoke to Kathy this morning," Mom said. "She and Doug are pushing up the date. They'll have a small ceremony in her apartment in a few weeks."

Poor Kathy. All those plans.

"What do you think, Ma, should I call her?" I asked. I prayed she'd say no.

Instead she said, "She'd probably feel good just to hear your voice. But if it's too hard for you to call today, I'm sure anytime this week would be fine."

I got up immediately and walked into the kitchen. Otherwise, I knew I'd be playing what I would say over and over in my head until I spoke to her. Nothing scary or unpleasant gets easier by anticipating it longer. This was not about a bottle of ketchup. This was real life.

The phone rang four times, then her answering machine went on. "Hi, burglars," said Kathy's familiar voice, "I'm not at home right now and probably won't be back for a few more hours. The jewels are in the night table to the right of my bed; the VCR's six years old and real heavy. It might not be worth the trip down the elevator. There's a beer in the fridge and some cookies in the pantry. See you later." Then the beep.

I hadn't thought of talking into a machine, but maybe this would be easier.

"Hi, Kathy, it's Erika. I'm sort of glad you're not there because I'm not really sure of what I want to say. All I know is that I'd do anything to make you feel better right now. It only takes an hour for me to get to you by bus and subway and ten seconds for you to reach me by phone. I'm available for ridiculous errands, menial chores, or just plain listening. I won't bother you. Just call when you feel like it."

All of a sudden I heard Kathy's voice. "Hold on, Erika. Let me shut off the machine." A second later she was back. "I'm screening my calls today, but I'd never not talk to you."

"Oh, Kathy, I'm so sorry." Hearing her voice filled my eyes with tears.

"I know, sweetie. You heard about the wedding?"

"Uh-huh. It'll be beautiful, Kathy. With some flowers, and the chairs moved back . . ."

"I don't care right now," she interrupted. "It'll be beautiful if my dad's there." Her voice broke. "I'm sorry, Erika. I love you madly, and I'm gonna count on you for a zillion things. I'm just not into wedding details right now."

"Of course. I just wanted to hear your voice. Oh, and maybe you should change your message."

"Why, you think they'll be pissed that there's no beer?" Kathy quipped, recovering quickly.

It was amazing. She'd known exactly what I was going to say.

I smiled. "Uh-huh. The last thing you

need is to be robbed by thieves who don't like you."

"OK. I'll change it tonight. By the way, thanks. I know it wasn't easy for you to make this call. Talk to you during the week. Bye."

"Poor Erika," sighed Allison later that night. "I know how much you've been looking forward to shopping for your fantasy dress."

I'd called Allison, in part because I wanted her sympathy. But not because of not getting a stupid dress.

"It's not the dress, Allison," I explained, talking to her like I would talk to a child. "It's just that my family can use a break from bad news. It was so nice to have something happy to look forward to."

It wasn't her fault that she didn't understand. She didn't have an uncle as wonderful as Uncle Frank. And she'd never lived under an ever-threatening dark cloud.

Then the rains came.

I came home from school Tuesday afternoon and saw Mom's car in the driveway. She was sitting having a cup of tea at the kitchen table with Gram and Grandpa.

"You OK?" I asked first, dropping my books on the counter. She nodded and I rattled on. "I'm glad you're home. Do you think you can

145

drive me to the shopping center? I need some new highlighters. It's so boring studying bio, but if I have a few new neon markers, I might manage to stay awake."

"I'll take you in a little while, Erika. Sit down for a minute." Her tone was ominous.

Just then I heard the toilet flush, and Dad walked out of the bathroom. I hadn't seen him since Sunday, and I was shocked at his appearance. He looked like he'd slept in his clothes, and his hair was sticking up at crazy angles. His face was puffy, and his eyes were all red. He needed a shave . . . and he smelled.

"I'm going up to take a shower," he mumbled, and left the room.

I looked to Mom, but she was staring after him. Gram blew her nose, and Grandpa leaned over to take my hand.

"Your dad didn't come home last night. He's had a rough few days," he said.

"Where was he?" I asked. "He looks terrible."

"He spent the night in jail, Erika. But he's home now," said my mom, regaining her composure.

My dad was back in the news. The TV anchor on channel 2 said that "in exchange for some measure of leniency, Stephen Gresham began telling prosecutors what he knew about the scandal. Rumor has it that by telling all he knows about his longtime friend and ally, Raymond Schuman, he was able to cut a deal with the district attorney." Now the headlines screamed that not only was he an extortionist, a public official on the take, he was also a snitch. As ugly as words like "racketeer," "bribery," "dirty contracts," and "crooked deals" had been, they had been related to business, and mostly I found their details too complicated to really follow. But to squeal on your best friend to save your own skin, that was easy to understand.

How was he going to sleep at night? How many people would he implicate to protect his sorry ass? Even the worst criminals lived by a code where keeping your mouth shut was the honorable thing to do. But not my dad.

My mom saw my face and read my mind. I really didn't care who heard what I was going to say. I heard chairs move back as Gram and Grandpa left the room.

It was quiet for a moment, then I asked, "Do you believe it? He's even worse than I thought. He's going to lose every friend he ever had. How can anyone trust him ever again?" I felt certain Mom and I were on the same side on this one.

"It's much more complicated than it looks,

honey. You shouldn't judge him so harshly for telling the truth. When you're in his position, you're not given much choice."

I couldn't believe she was sticking up for him. Mom, my nauseatingly play-fair-and-square Mom, was trying to tell me that ratting on your friends is the right thing to do.

"Telling the truth because it suits your purposes is a little different than telling the truth to do the right thing."

"Take it easy, Erika. You're smart enough by this time to know that not everything you read and hear on the news is exactly what's happening. Whatever your father is telling the prosecutor, he's telling for the right reasons." Her cheeks were flushed, her eyes were watery, and her voice was almost shrill, entering a range I'd never heard before. This is what Mom looks and sounds like when she's approaching out of control, I thought. As often as I had wanted to shake her for keeping her emotions in check, I felt uneasy seeing her facade begin to crack.

"Did you expect him to take all the blame by himself? Is that what you'd want him to do? Lie and say it was all his idea?" She was yelling now and glaring at me as if I was the one to blame.

"I don't know. I always thought it was wrong to snitch on your friends." I purposely lowered my voice and spoke slowly. It was a trick I learned from Mom. That's how she'd get my attention when I'd be real angry with her. The softer her voice sounded, the harsher and meaner mine did. "How can he tell on Uncle Ray?"

Mom didn't answer. She looked up and saw my father standing in the doorway.

"This is my job, Charlotte," said my father to her wearily. He poured himself a glass of juice and sat down opposite me at the kitchen table. My mother glanced at me once more and left the room.

I sat back in my chair and folded my hands across my chest.

He put his elbows on the table and dropped his face in his hands. He started to rub his temples. "The world of politics is a world of making deals." He waited a long moment. "If you're not immersed in that world of money and power and business and compromise, you're not familiar with the methods politicians use to find solutions to their problems. Giving people what they want in return for getting something that you need is the way it works. It's not right or wrong—it just is."

"You're not wrong? I can't believe you're not wrong. You didn't even tell Mom what you were doing!" For a split second I flashed on the old people-who-live-in-glass-houses cliché. I'd cheated, I'd lied, and I hadn't told her either. I curled my toes hard inside my sneakers to force myself to refocus my thoughts. I'd waited too long for this opportunity to waste it. He looked pitiful but I didn't care. We were in the same room alone for once, and he was going to answer some of my questions.

"I knew that once I told your mother what was going on, she'd be a part of it. In my warped mind I figured I was protecting her." He smiled sadly. "I don't expect you to understand why I said and did what I did. I just hoped that you'd have a little more patience than the average person and realize that maybe there's more to this story than what you hear on TV. Don't forgive me or support me, if you can't, but don't condemn me without the benefit of a doubt."

I wanted to share what I was feeling with my real father, not this stinking, squealing impostor. I remembered how warm and safe I used to feel inside his hug. I blinked my eyes to make the memory disappear.

"What does Uncle Ray say about all this? Is *he* giving you the benefit of the doubt?"

My father didn't look up from the table.

"Uncle Ray would do the same thing," he said firmly. "Look, Erika. They give you no choice. Tell the whole truth . . . or go to jail for twenty-five years. Either-or. Nothing in between."

I didn't say a word.

"That's their definition of plea bargaining. It's a negotiation," he laughed bitterly. "Give them the information they want, and in return they'll give you back a piece of what's left of your life. One hand washes the other, they said." He shook his head.

"Couldn't you have . . . ," I began, then stopped midsentence. Dad was looking at me, but I knew he didn't see me. He looked like a bear who had been shot . . . wounded and dazed. No matter what I was going to say, he wouldn't hear me. Yelling at him would be like kicking someone when they're down for the count. How ironic. Dad was three times my size, but I couldn't pick on him because I had the unfair advantage.

"*I . . . had . . . no . . . choice,*" he said very slowly, through clenched teeth. He put his head down on the table over his clasped palms. It was like he forgot I was even there.

I had this picture in my mind of the prosecutor wearing a helmet and shiny boots, whipping my dad into telling all he knew. But this was New York, not Nazi Germany. I got up from the table, picked up my books, and started for the stairs.

Up in my room I thought about how I'd be forty-one before my father would get out of prison if he didn't agree to plea-bargain. Then I got into the hottest shower I could stand, to force myself to stop thinking about anything at all.

Three Advil did nothing to dull the pounding in my head that night. I wondered if Mom could write a note to Mr. Johnson explaining why I was going to fail his bio test. "Due to circumstances beyond her control," she could say, "Erika's brain was nowhere to be found last night. She got new neon markers to highlight her notes, but unfortunately she couldn't distinguish an important fact from a doodle in the margins." It wasn't funny. I hadn't the slightest idea of where my mind was or what I was thinking when I attempted to study—all I knew was I didn't know enough to pass that test. It was 1:50 A.M. the last time I looked at the clock. But I should've known better than to expect that sleep would take me to a better place.

I was playing tennis in the country somewhere. The court was gray and pockmarked and weeds were coming through the cracks in the cement. It was hot and humid and the air smelled like sweaty old sneakers. I couldn't identify my opponent, but the stands were filled with people all dressed in the same light blue jumpsuit. I aced my first serve.

"That's my girl," I heard my father yell. "I taught her everything she knows." He turned to the man next to him. "You should've been there when she called that last ball out. She's a winner, my girl, one way or the other."

I glanced around and saw he was washing his hands. The windows in the building behind the bleachers all had bars.

It was just Matt's style not to tell anyone that he was coming home. People like him think they're above common courtesy because they're too busy making the world a better place. How he'd think something like telling your mother you're coming home for the weekend would mess up his moral compass, I have no idea.

We were just finishing dinner Friday night, the only night Gram and Grandpa, Mom and me sat down and ate with Dad. The conversation was usually livelier than the rest of the week, although we never discussed Dad's case at the dinner table. We looked like a regular family on Friday nights, eating chicken or brisket, noodle pudding and string beans, and always the world's best chicken soup. Dad and Grandpa would be arguing about why the Knicks lost the night before, Mom would be asking me about my weekend plans, and Grandma would be in all her glory, feeding food to her family. She had just brought out tea and the lightest lemony sponge cake when the doorbell rang.

"Go answer the door, Willard," Gram said as she set down the teapot. Immediately the mood changed. Whoever rang the bell brought in with him the world we were doing our best to keep out. We all waited quietly, listening to hear who was intruding on our privacy.

"Well, son of a gun! Come on in," we heard Grandpa exclaim. "Cleo, Charlotte, guess who's here?"

Mom and Gram both got up and ran to the door. It was obviously someone welcome. Dad and I waited, picking at our dessert.

"You expecting anyone?" I asked, knowing he wasn't but wanting to end the awkward silence between us. We hadn't spoken since the kitchen table conversation three days before.

"Nope, you?" he answered, humoring me.

"No." I strained to think of something else to say but came up empty.

"What a wonderful surprise!" we heard Gram exclaim.

"Oh, honey, we've just finished eating. Why didn't you tell us you were coming?" Mom asked.

"No problem, just sit down. I'll make you a plate in one minute," said Gram.

"Well, it's obviously no friend of mine," Dad said dryly.

Another time I might have appreciated the black humor, but this was too true to be funny. My heart started to beat faster when I realized who it was at the door. Only Matt would cause such a commotion. Another time I'd be up in a flash to give him the biggest greeting of all. But Dad and I both had our reasons for remaining seated.

A minute later he appeared. It was a chilly night but he wore no jacket. Just an Elton John concert T-shirt from 1988 that was all stretched out from hundreds of washings, a pair of Levi's that were fashionably old but unfashionably not holey or shredded, and a pair of basketball sneakers that I remembered he got when I was in junior high school. He could've passed for one of the people he helps at the soup kitchen. He carried just a small knapsack, which I was sure was packed with books, carob chips, his reading glasses, and probably this month's *Omni* magazine. For sure there'd be no change of clothes or extra money in case of emergency.

"Hey, Erika—what's the matter, I'm not important enough to get up for? You think I traveled all this way to be dissed by my little sister? Get over here," he said, stretching his arms out to me.

I was surprised at the warmth of his greeting. It had always been me asking him for a hug and him, a bit overwhelmed, hugging me back. Then I realized why: he was making this big deal about me to prolong dealing with his father. Dad just sat there watching. Then, I guess to avoid the horrible possibility that Matt wouldn't even say hello to him, he got up and walked around to where I was sitting.

"Hi, son, it's good to see you. It feels like a long time since we've been together." I noticed that there were tiny beads of perspiration on Dad's forehead. He put out his hand to shake Matt's hand. Smart move, I thought, that he didn't move in for a hug.

"It's been a while," agreed Matt quietly. He returned Dad's handshake and immediately turned his attention back to me.

"Come here, Erika. What's the story here? I don't recall ever having to beg for a hug." Matt's eyes locked with mine, and I read what they were saying: "Erika, help me out. Come here so he'll move away."

I stood up, stretched out my arms, and smiled. I'd get him out of his handshake, but I'd be damned if I was going to walk over to make it that easy.

He ran over to where I was standing and gave me the longest embrace of our existence.

"I missed you. Can't quite figure out why," he said softly, almost losing his big-brother sarcastic tone.

"I missed you, too," I whispered back. "And I know exactly why." I stared right at him till he turned away. It was like we'd had a whole long argument and I came out on top.

We took our seats around the table once more. Gram made Matt a plate that must've weighed ten pounds, and he ate every last crumb. Not an easy task while answering all of her questions fired at him at supersonic speed.

"To what do we owe such a visit? I thought you forgot you had a family by this time.

"So how's that project going? Your professor like you?

"Do you ever pick your head up from those books? There's such a thing as fun, you know.

"Meet any nice girls?

"Can't you spare a few dollars to buy some new clothes?"

Remarkably, he answered them all with good humor.

At about eleven o'clock we all went up to bed. Matt slept on a cot squeezed into my room. I was happy to see him, but it was happiness mixed with disappointment and lots more anger than I realized.

I shut the light, and we both got into bed. I gave him a minute to start a conversation, and when he didn't, I began.

"You could've asked Dad how he was doing, instead of ignoring him all night," I said.

"Ignoring him was the kindest way I could possibly handle him now," he answered. "It's only because of you and Mom that I kept my mouth shut. If I started, I don't know what I'd say." His voice sounded cold. "It's not my job to make this whole thing easier for him. If he wants to ruin his life, let him. I'm just completely turned off by how he's handled himself during this whole fiasco."

I didn't answer. He sounded arrogant and selfish.

"You know, Matt, I think we were a pretty close family before this all happened. Just because you're pissed at Dad or Mom or me even, doesn't give you the right to ignore us. You're right, what Dad did *was* disgusting, but you pretending we don't exist is a pretty lame way of handling it." I couldn't believe how calm I sounded. I was glad the lights were out so I couldn't see his face.

He didn't say anything for a long time. Then he asked me how Mom was managing, how my friends were, how I felt about living at Gram's. I talked on and on, about how lousy I was doing in school, how hard it was falling asleep, how I missed having MTV. I told him about Greg, about Uncle Frank, about Dad testifying against Uncle Ray. When I was done, it was silent in the room. Suddenly my heart sank. What if he'd fallen asleep?

A minute later I heard him get off his cot and come over to sit on the edge of my bed. My eyes were used to the dark now, and I could see him looking down at me. His arms were stiffly at his side, his hands, fists on the bed. He looked so lost and troubled that I felt whatever hostility I was harboring slowly evaporate.

"You want me to give you the chills?" Just like me, he loved having his back and his arms given the goose bumps. I had paid off countless debts and earned scores of ice-cream cones through the years performing this talent. "This one's on me." I reached for his arm.

Instead he took my hand and placed it

in his palm, then covered it with his other hand.

"No, no. No rewards for my acting like an asshole."

I sat up next to him and leaned my head on his shoulder. He curled his arm around me and tilted his head so it rested on mine.

"You know I've always prided myself on never taking the easy way out," he began. "I get off on setting impossible goals, and reaching them in half the time it would take someone else. But this thing with Dad"—his voice broke—"I can't do the hard thing. Forget about understanding it or forgiving him, I can't even be angry the right way. So I bury it. It's hard to believe, but I hardly even think about it most days." He stopped. "The only problem is that to do that I have to forget about you and Mom, too. I had to come this weekend because I felt so guilty I couldn't stand it anymore."

For an instant I flashed on how we could trade guilt stories if I told him about the tennis tournament. Then I decided it was too big a risk. If he couldn't forgive Dad, what would he think of me?

"That's OK, Matt. If I wasn't home, I'd probably do the same exact thing." I didn't move, closing my eyes to enjoy how sweet it was to lean on him. It was the kind of comfortable that's impossible for just one person to feel, and I prayed he wouldn't change positions. He didn't.

"I doubt it, Erika. You're not selfish enough." He squeezed my shoulder. "If I've made this tougher on you than it already was, I'm sorry. From now on, I promise I'll be available. I'll do my share with Mom, too."

I knew better than to ask him what he was going to do about Dad. A person can only do the best he can do.

I sighed. "It's nice having you back, Matt." I closed my eyes and felt so relaxed I must've dozed off.

I felt Matt gently lay my head on the pillow. I pretended I was sleeping and allowed him to carefully pull the covers up to my chin and then neatly fold them over. He bent down and kissed me on the cheek, and went back to his cot. I smiled in the darkness, feeling more peaceful than I had in a long time. The horror of the scandal was far from over, but at least now I wouldn't be facing it totally alone.

The next day I bought a card to send to Greg. This time I had no trouble finding the perfect one. On the front was a blond little girl with her hair in two braids, sitting on top of about fifty soup bowls on a comfortable flowered living room chair. When you opened it up, it just said, "Life is just a chair of bowlies." I wrote,

> Dear Greg,
> This about describes my mental state. Never before has my life been so full of "bowlies." This week alone I have been surprised by, furious at, and felt sorry for every member of my family. Life was a lot less complicated when I either loved or hated them!
> Even though it's frustrating not being able to spend time together, it feels great just knowing you're there. I'm sorry I can't call but a long-distance charge on my grandmother's telephone bill might just push her over the edge. As it is, I piss her off twelve different ways, even when I'm on my best behavior.
> I hope everything's going OK with you. When will you find out about being captain of the soccer team? You know you have my vote . . .
> Summer's just around the corner.
>
> Love,
> Erika

Exactly five days later I got a card back. It had two elephants on the front; one was crouching down and the other was trying to lift his leg over the other elephant to get to the other side. When you opened the card, it just said, "I can't get over you." He just wrote a few words, but they kept me going for the rest of the week.

Dear Erika,

I truly can't get over you. Anyone else in your position would take advantage of my sympathetic ear and unload every miserable complaint and be perfectly justified. But you're so mature and optimistic, it's amazing. I guess that's one reason why you have the captain of the Somerfield H.S. soccer team thinking about you all the time!

I'm making it my mission to try to help you have the summer you deserve.

Love,
Greg

While being called mature and optimistic wasn't exactly love letter material, I couldn't have been happier. And imagining exactly what he meant by his last line was more than enough to fuel my daydreams for the next sixty-three days.

CHAPTER 8

New York Tribune

Raymond Schuman hanged himself in the bedroom of his home, amid widening allegations of corruption against him. The suicide took place two weeks after Stephen Gresham, in exchange for some measure of leniency, began telling prosecutors what he knew of the State corruption scandal. Schuman was facing almost certain indictment in New York's worst corruption scandal in decades. An unidentified source close to Schuman said he was an ambitious man who, when he suddenly saw his hard-won world collapse, couldn't face further public humiliation.

WE FOUND OUT that Uncle Ray hanged himself on the evening news. Dad wasn't home yet, Mom and Gram were in the kitchen, and Grandpa and I were just settling down to hear the 7:00 broadcast. In the last few weeks Dad's scandal had moved down the news ladder in importance to item nine or ten, so we rarely gave the TV our full attention till almost ten minutes into the show. But tonight the news began with a picture of Uncle Ray, smiling last year at the governor's victory party.

"Amid increasing despondency that paralleled the growing focus upon him in investigations into municipal corruption, Raymond Schuman, the former powerful commissioner of the State Education Department, hanged himself in the bedroom closet of his Long Island home just hours ago. His wife and children were in the house at the time. Apparently, the family housekeeper found him and called 911. He was pronounced dead on arrival at North Shore Hospital. There is widespread speculation that yesterday's grand jury testimony of longtime friend Stephen Gresham was directly related to today's tragic incident. Gresham revealed how, for the last six years, Schuman had initiated and directed a multi-million-dollar bribery scheme from his office at the State Education Department. The governor, the Schuman family, and Stephen Gresham, presently residing at an undisclosed location, were all unavailable for comment."

Grandpa and I sat there. The announcer

was now on to the devastation resulting from an earthquake in Iran. I felt for his hand and for the first time found it cold and clammy. My face felt hot, and my head was pounding double time.

"We have to tell them," I whispered, motioning toward the kitchen. "I can't, Grandpa. I can't tell Mommy that Uncle Ray is dead." I started to cry.

Grandpa let me sob quietly for a minute. Then he said, "Are you OK to be left alone? I want you to sit right here while I go into the kitchen and tell your mother and grandmother. But I won't go to them yet, if you need me here."

I walked over to the dining room table and picked up a napkin to blow my nose. "I'm OK. How are you going to tell them?" I looked at him now standing tall, making his way toward the kitchen, and wondered, in his seven decades of life, how many hard things like this he'd had to do. I remember thinking how calm and brave he was, followed quickly by how really he had no choice. I realized then that sometimes life forces you to be brave by taking away your options. All you can do is stand there and live through it.

I heard Grandpa's voice talking so quietly I couldn't make out the words. I expected to hear yelling and screaming but heard an unfamiliar moaning instead. Then Gram's voice.

"Where's Stephen? Is he still at the lawyer's? He shouldn't be alone when he hears."

"I'll call the lawyer; you take care of Charlotte," I heard Grandpa say.

"Come here, sweetheart. You're not too big to let me hold you," said Gram's voice. I heard a chair being pushed back and pictured the scene. I wasn't ready to see Mom's face, so I just sat on the couch figuring sooner or later they'd come into the living room. My mind was racing. "His family was home at the time." How could he let Carole, Susan, and Emily see him like that? How could anything be so bad you kill yourself? We'd had a handyman once who said, when Mom called him about the latest part of the house that was falling apart, "There's a solution to every problem. You just need the patience to look for it." He wasn't so great at finding the solutions himself, but his words always stayed in my mind. Just then I remembered other words, this time said by Dad, whenever I looked down in the dumps. "You look like you just lost your best friend," he would say, trying to shake me out of my mood. Now I was going to see just what that looks like.

The kitchen door swung open, and the three of them came into the living room.

"He left the lawyer's office about a half hour ago. He didn't know anything up to then. The secretary's pretty sure he was on his way home," Grandpa said to Gram.

Mom came over and gave me a hug. I started to really cry then, and so did she.

"My poor baby," she said through her tears. "You're so young to go through all of this."

"We're all too young to go through this," Gram said. "But we have each other and our health, and that's what matters. The rest we'll survive."

It sounded like she was talking as much to convince herself as to give us courage. I wasn't sure which hurt worse—my grief over Uncle Ray's dying, or my fear of seeing Dad's face.

Suddenly we heard Dad's car in the driveway. Mom left me and ran to the front door.

"Oh God," she said, "I hope he already knows 'cause I don't think I'll be able to tell him if he doesn't." She stood at the door, taking deep breaths, wiping her eyes, and blowing her nose with the remnants of a soggy tissue. She opened the door and walked out onto the porch.

"Charlotte, it's cold. Put on a jacket," Gram called after her.

"Leave her alone, Cleo. I guarantee she's not cold," Grandpa said.

We heard Mom talking softly. Then we heard a noise I can only compare to the sound Allison's cat once made when I accidentally ran over his tail while rocking in her rocking chair. It was almost unrecognizable as human, so sharp and loud and full of pain. I saw Grandma shudder and Grandpa nervously run his fingers through his hair. I wanted to put my fingers in my ears, but I knew that sound would travel through stone.

My father's arm was looped over my mother's shoulders, as if she were carrying him into the house. He was crying, and his face was wet with tears.

"Shhh, Stephen," said my mom, pushing his hair away from his face, using the tissues Gram had just handed her to wipe his face.

"It wasn't your fault. There was nothing you could do. How could you have known he'd be so desperate?"

"If I didn't know, I should've," Dad said, pulling away from her. "Whoever thought he'd go through with it? He always talked crazy just for the effect, to get everyone's attention. Whoever thought he'd be stupid enough to actually do it?" He started to sob, this time more quietly.

It was even worse than tragic. Uncle Ray had mentioned suicide, and Dad hadn't believed him. At that moment I felt sorrier for my father than anyone else in the world. To feel responsible for the death of someone you loved must be one of life's most horrible feelings. Trials and headlines, even jail, seemed no big deal by comparison. At least you knew one day it'd be finished. What Uncle Ray did would hurt his family and friends forever.

"I gotta go upstairs," said Dad, suddenly aware of Grandma, Grandpa, and me in the room. "I gotta lie down. Charlotte, just let me be for a while, OK?" We heard the door slam.

Mom started to follow him, but Grandpa took her arm. "Give him some time, Charlotte. He'll need you for the rest of his life; now he needs to be alone."

"Oh, Daddy," Mom said, crumpling in Grandpa's arms. "Will this ever end?"

"Yes, Charlotte," he said, rocking slowly side to side, holding Mom tightly. "I promise, I promise."

The next few days passed in a blur. Because of the press, Mom and Dad couldn't even go to the funeral. Because of the allegations blaming Dad's testimony for the suicide, Mom couldn't even call to speak to Uncle Ray's family. We watched the news on every channel and bought every newspaper. The story was made for the press and TV. They showed footage of

Uncle Ray's public life going back twenty years. The pictures revealed a man who loved his public position and the power it brought. There were photos of the family, of our cottages at the beach, and of Dad and him.

"The trial of defendants involved in the State Education Department scandal scheduled to start in the next six weeks is expected to reveal a darker side to Raymond Schuman," said an anchorman, "a man who led a secret life of intense greed and feared losing it all by having his corrupt activities discovered."

We sat there "at an undisclosed location," sharing the events one step removed but still, as they say on TV, up close and personal.

Every once in a while Mom would say things like, "Carole and the girls know, Stephen. They know what he did had nothing to do with you." Or "You must be strong now, to save your own life. You just have to tell the truth and deal with the consequences. Whatever they are, they'll be easier to handle than this."

He listened but he didn't answer. Before, he was a part of a whole. Now he was alone. He had to face whatever lay ahead and shoulder the blame—alone. If I thought he was distant and remote from me before, now it was like I was invisible.

Even Greg couldn't help make things better. I called him the day after the suicide.

"Geez, Erika, this story gets curiouser and curiouser. Is it true they found him in a closet? How long was he in there, do you think?"

"*A Current Affair* will give you a play-by-play description of what happened," I snapped, wanting only to get off the phone before I blamed him for not always being the perfect answer to my every need. "They specialize in close-ups of blood and guts."

"Hey, I'm sorry," he said contritely. "I guess the TV coverage made me forget that this whole thing's not a soap opera . . . It's your life."

"Don't worry about it," I said tiredly. "I just wanted to hear your voice."

"I'll call you in a few days to see how you're doing. And I promise to not be such a jerk."

In school it was worse. Now that the scandal had a dead body, a funeral that even the governor attended, and my father's testimony mentioned as the main reason for the suicide, the story took on a different aura— the *Enquirer, Hard Copy, Inside Edition* kind of aura. Kids who never said hello to me before were either trying to suck up to me in that let-me-touch-the-hand-that-touched-the-hand kind of way, or they stopped talking when I came near.

"You poor girl. This must be so hard for you," said Stacey, her voice dripping with insincerity. "How's your father feeling?"

"He's holding up OK," I lied. "Thanks for asking." Bitch.

"Well, if there's anything I can do, just ask," she said sweetly.

Don't talk to me ever again, I thought to myself. Don't look at me, don't even think about me. That would be all I'd want from you. Wait till she finds out I'm not playing tennis next year. She'll send my dad a thank-you note.

"Why do you let her bother you?" said Allison later that night on the phone. "She's so sick, she wishes she were you, the center of attention; any kind of attention."

"I wish she were me, too," I said miserably. "All this couldn't happen to a nicer person than Stacey."

Without any joy Mom and I went through the motions of shopping for a dress for Kathy's revised wedding. I found an emerald green silk suit with a peplum jacket and a straight, short skirt. It wasn't strapless or satin, but it was sophisticated, and I knew Kathy would approve.

As it turned out, Kathy sacrificed nothing

by having an intimate wedding at home. Uncle Frank joked and drank and had a wonderful time. The rest of us took our cue from him and celebrated even more.

There wasn't a person who wasn't moved by the ceremony. Kathy and Doug had written most of it themselves. The rabbi of our temple officiated, and I saw firsthand why Kathy was always encouraging me to attend Friday night services. (I wasn't much for organized religion, though, and couldn't imagine going to temple if I wasn't forced to.)

Rabbi Arnold Beckman was the kind of guy you'd never believe was a rabbi. You could see his friends probably called him Arnie. He didn't have that disapproving air that I thought was a prerequisite for the job. He had blue eyes, curly gray hair, and the unique gift of making you feel, when you spoke to him, that he was intensely interested in every word you had to say. The kids in the neighborhood told me that he loved rock and roll music, was a sports fanatic, and unlike Allison's rabbi, who told the whole congregation how much he loved her at her confirmation and then didn't even recognize her three months later when she ran into him at the movies, knew everyone by name. His wasn't a canned speech; this was a carefully tailored sermon directed solely to Kathy and Doug. The way he talked about compromise and forgiveness, sharing, and depending on one another, it was like you never heard of such concepts before. When he was done, we had to consciously keep from applauding.

When we left, I hugged her and said, "I hope you realize you got exactly the wedding I wished for you."

"Thank you, Erika," she said, her eyes sparkling. "We all needed today." They left the next day for a ten-day honeymoon in Hawaii. It was Uncle Frank's wedding present to them. Smart man that he was, he knew Kathy would never leave him for ten days unless it was booked and unrefundable. Kind, gentle, unselfish man that he was, no one knew till the following week how bad he was really feeling.

Uncle Frank was admitted to the hospital exactly two weeks after the wedding. The cancer was spreading fast now, and there wasn't much the doctors could do but keep him comfortable. He had an IV tube that dripped small doses of morphine into his skinny arm.

I went to the hospital on the weekends. Watching Uncle Frank grow thinner and weaker energized my hostility toward my father. There was Kathy losing a dad she loved so much, and there was me wishing mine would disappear. I found myself imagining my dad trading places with Uncle Frank, then got so uncomfortable with the thought, I couldn't stand it. It's not that I felt Dad deserved to die, I just thought there'd probably be less grief per square inch if it were him lying in that bed.

The next Monday there was a note left on my desk in homeroom. I recognized the handwriting as Mr. DaMaio's. I opened it and read,

> To the player I thought was a shoo-in to receive the Most Outstanding Senior Award next year,
>
> Say it's not so. . . . Since when do I have to hear through much-less-than-reliable sources that you're quitting the tennis team? Doesn't sound like you. One, to quit and two, not to give me the courtesy of an explanation. Your schedule shows you're free fourth period. I'll be waiting in my office.
>
> Ron

It had to be Stacey who told him. But who told her? Just what I needed right now—a confrontation. He was right, of course, I should have notified him first. Ever since the tennis tournament I had tried to avoid any contact

176

with him. I knew he hadn't seen how I had played the match, but that didn't make it any easier for me to be around him. Well, I thought, taking a deep breath and walking into the phys ed office, here goes nothing.

Mr. DaMaio glanced up from his desk. He stood up and motioned for me to take the seat opposite him. He wasn't smiling.

"So?" he asked. "Enquiring minds want to know. Is it true that you're going to quit the team?"

"I meant to come talk to you," I began. "I'm sorry. It's just that my life's been so crazy lately that I didn't have a moment . . ."

"Uh-huh." No smile. "Go on."

I couldn't believe he wasn't even going to try to understand why I didn't feel like playing. All this time I could've milked what was happening at home to get out of all kinds of work in school, and I didn't. Now that I needed some compassion, all I was getting was a scowl.

"You know, I've been living with my grandparents. And my father's been indicted on charges . . . Well, I figure next year he'll be in jail. And I doubt that I'll be in the mood to play tennis . . ." I waited but he didn't say a word. I decided to use the heavy artillery.

"I'm too ashamed to stand up there in front of everybody, Mr. DaMaio," I said softly. "I can't see how I can stay focused. I don't want to disgrace the team . . ."

"So don't!" he interrupted. "What's this garbage about not being in the mood . . . being too ashamed . . . not able to stay focused? Those are fake reasons. One, moods change minute to minute, and now you're projecting how you're going to feel in the fall. Two, as far as I know, shame taints the shamee—it's not inherited. And three, it seems to me all you're focusing on is you and yourself. You're not thinking about a group of girls who've worked hard and finally moved up to compete in Division A. What's going to happen to them?"

Not only wasn't I being excused, I was being accused of being selfish. I didn't know what to say. Not to worry, Mr. DaMaio wasn't finished.

"I pegged you for a winner, Erika. Since you were a freshman, you've been committed to doing the best job you possibly could. Winners overcome adversity; they don't lie down and roll over. If I were you, I'd think about what's really keeping me from playing, and I'd retire that bunch of excuses you came in with."

My cheeks felt hot. "I really don't know what you're talking about, Mr. DaMaio. I told you the truth. I hated the feeling I had when I played in the tournament, after everybody knew . . ."

"But you won," he interrupted.

No, I didn't! I screamed inside. I cheated. I lied. You'd hate me if you knew the truth!

I went on, "I felt empty." I felt sick inside. How much harder could telling the truth be?

Mr. DaMaio stood up to signal the end of our meeting.

"Don't decide anything now. I'll accept your resignation when you come in and tell me the real reason why you don't want to play next year." He'd completely ignored what I just said.

I gathered up my books and slung my pocketbook over my shoulder. What did he think my real reason was?

CHAPTER 9

Long Island Weekly, *Editorial*

The ongoing investigation of corruption in New York State government is likely to go on for months, revealing an appalling picture of self-enriching influence peddling by politicians. What disturbs us is the option, taken by defendants like Stephen Gresham, of testifying against others in return for a lighter sentence. We see this plea bargaining as a symbol of lax justice. The majority of people who work for government are honest, dedicated, and committed, and those who have violated the public trust and pocket the spoils belong in jail, regardless of how valuable their testimony might be.

I DON'T THINK there was one person at Uncle Frank's funeral who wouldn't truly miss him now that he was gone. I mean, I know most people don't wish death on anyone, but the few funerals I've been to in my life taught me that people go to them for lots of reasons other than sorrow. When Allison's grandmother died, I went to be there for her. When old Mr. Pintchik from down the block died, Mom and Dad went to his funeral out of respect, because it was the right thing to do, Mom said. And when Uncle Ray died, the papers said there were hundreds of people there. I'm sure he hadn't known them all. Many came, Grandpa said as he watched the crowds on TV, because they were afraid not to. But when a sweet, gentle man like Uncle Frank dies, there's really no reason to come to his funeral unless you just want to be there.

The day passed in a blur. After the service we went to the cemetery and then back to Aunt Shirley's house. There are two things I'll never understand about days like this. First, how you get back in the car and just drive away, leaving a person you love alone under a few shovelfuls of dirt. And second, how grief gives you an appetite large enough to demolish platters of bagels and cheeses and fish and cakes the moment you get back into the house. I helped Mom clear the table, put out fresh food, and make another pot of coffee.

"Can I give you a hand?" my dad asked as I tried to open the side door in the kitchen to put out a huge plastic garbage bag full of dirty paper goods.

"No thanks, I've got it," I said flatly. For some reason, since I'd heard about Uncle Frank, I had even less than no use for Dad. It wasn't that he said or did anything wrong; it was just that he was there. Paunchy and sweaty, trying too hard—everything about him bothered me.

"Don't be so stubborn," he said, holding the door open. "I'm just trying to help." If he noticed my tone, he ignored it.

"I'm not being stubborn," I said louder than I meant to. "If I want your help, I'll ask for it." A few of the people milling about the kitchen looked up. Even Kathy looked a little surprised that those words came out of me.

Damn him, I thought. Just what Kathy needed today—to see me fighting with my dad. I wished he'd fall off the face of the earth.

In a quiet but surprisingly firm voice he said, "Erika, can I speak to you for a minute?" His jaw muscle was twitching, a sure sign that something was brewing inside.

"Can't it wait?" Maybe later I'd have more patience for the lecture I could probably quote by heart: No matter how mad you are, now's no time to show it. . . . Tell me what's on your mind, don't snap at me. . . . I will not tolerate disrespect. . . . Blah, blah, blah.

"No, I don't think so," he said, taking my elbow in his hand and pushing me toward the pantry. The few people sitting around the kitchen table glanced in our direction, then got up to go sit in the living room.

"What is it?" I said. "I want to go sit with Kathy."

"What you want to do is not my concern right now," Dad said angrily. "I don't know who you think you're talking to in that arrogant tone, but I won't tolerate it anymore. I've been excusing your attitude for too long now. It's got to stop."

"*You've* been excusing?" I said incredulously. "That's funny. I've done nothing for you to excuse. In fact, I think I've been incredibly civil considering . . ." I folded my hands across my chest and dared him to continue.

"Considering what? I didn't commit murder, Erika, and I did nothing intentionally to hurt anyone. Do you think I'm not being punished enough? That I need your disrespect to remind me of what happened? We're a family, for God's sake. I can't think of anything *you* could do that would make me give up on *you.*"

I rubbed my brow to avoid his eyes. Implicit

in his tone was the memory of the tennis match. Here was his chance to retaliate, to bully me with some snide comment. My body tensed, but he didn't say a word.

"Maybe you're more forgiving than me," I said. "Maybe you're just a better person!" My voice was harsh, and my hands were trembling. If we were anywhere else, I would have had the luxury of screaming. I was making him feel wretched—and I was glad.

Suddenly he made a move toward me, then he changed his mind and leaned heavily backward onto the kitchen counter. "Go if you want," he said bitterly. "Just don't convince yourself that you deserve to get away with *your* transgressions because you're suffering the effects of mine. That's not the way it works."

I shrugged and pretended I didn't understand what he was referring to. "I'll try to remember that," I said, making my way out of the kitchen, "before I commit my next crime."

I walked into the living room and took a seat next to Kathy on the couch. I looked in the direction of the kitchen and wrinkled up my nose, sure that she'd pick up on my disgust. If I thought I'd get support, I was mistaken.

"Look, Erika, you keep asking if there's anything you can do for me," she said softly. "Well, there is one thing. You can find something better to do with your anger than lash out at your father in front of people. I want you to go talk to Rabbi Beckman."

"*What?*"

"I hate to see you this way. Promise me you'll call."

I made a face, but I could see she was serious.

"OK, OK. I promise. I'll make an appointment to speak with him next week."

It took ten days for me to make the call. I waited till I was alone in the house. The whole idea actually scared me—I mean, how much sense does it make to go to a place devoted to worshipping God to talk about how I hated my father? And aside from the fact that I honestly believed this was a situation where no advice could really help, it was hard to imagine opening up to a stranger. I remembered that Allison's sister had gone to a psychologist once a few years back, and she'd loved it.

"It's the best," she'd said. "You walk in, tell the absolute truth no matter how brutal, have someone listen with a hundred percent of their attention and then compliment you on your honesty. No 'you should'ves,' no 'how could yous,' just 'hmm, hmm, I see' or 'what happened next?' I'm not really sure how it all works, but I know it does, if you go to the right person."

I hoped Rabbi Beckman was the right person. I wondered whether my almost nonexistent religious background would work against me. I just prayed I wouldn't freak him out with my sins. His secretary told me the rabbi would get back to me to set up an appointment. Not even an hour later the phone rang.

"Hello, Erika, this is Rabbi Beckman," he said.

"Oh, hi, Rabbi," I answered, "thanks for getting back to me so fast. Uh, I was wondering if I could come in sometime to see you. Things have been a bit hairy in my house for the past few months, and I thought . . . well actually my cousin Kathy thought, it'd be a good idea to talk to you."

Brilliant. He'll definitely be impressed with my extensive vocabulary—hairy! How profound.

"Is tomorrow afternoon at four o'clock good for you?" he asked.

"That would be great. I really appreciate it. It shouldn't take too long . . ."

Rabbi Beckman laughed. "You know how long our conversation's going to last a day before you get here. That's pretty good." Then his tone changed. "I have nothing scheduled till six. And that's only dinner. If we're not done, we'll meet again, don't worry."

I began to relax. "I'm a little nervous about coming. I'm not really sure why I'm even bothering you."

"Erika, it's a compliment to me that you've sought me out. Do me a favor. Don't plan your agenda, don't organize your thoughts, just come in and let's see what happens."

It was as if he'd read my mind. Already I was making a mental list of what to talk about first and what to be careful not to mention.

"OK, Rabbi, I'll see you tomorrow at four. Thanks again."

The next day after school I walked the mile and a half to the temple. I had so much nervous energy, I made the trip in record time. That morning I'd told Gram I was going to the library to work on a paper.

"Do you want Grandpa to pick you up when you're done?" she asked.

"Thanks. I'll call if I need him," I answered, kissing her on the cheek as I went out the door. She wasn't really a bad person, I thought for the thousandth time in four months, we're just so different. I wonder what she would've thought of my talking to the rabbi.

The secretary directed me to Rabbi Beckman's office. The door was closed, and I knocked, suddenly scared all over again.

"Come on in, Erika," he called out. "I'll be with you in a second."

His office was done in shades of gray and burgundy, at once warm and comfortable yet seriously elegant. I was glad he was on the phone, giving me time to decide where to sit, to check out the photos of his family, to catch my breath.

He got off the phone quickly and came around the desk to shake my hand. He pressed down the intercom on his desk and said, "Betty, please hold my calls. I'll get back to everyone before I leave tonight."

I was impressed and intimidated at the same moment. "So?" he said with a smile. Instead of going back behind his desk, he sat down in the seat right next to me.

"This is very hard," I began. "I'm having a tough time trusting anyone these days."

He nodded. "Look, Erika, I think I'd make a pretty good friend if you give me a chance. I can't promise you perfect answers, but I can promise you confidentiality and that I'll always be here."

I took a deep breath and blurted out, "I hate my father for what he's done to me and my family. I always thought he was the neatest guy in the world, and now that I see the truth, I can't stand being around him. I'm mean to him, and I'm scared that I'm never going to feel any different." There, it was out. I half expected lightning and thunder.

Rabbi Beckman didn't show any reaction. When he did speak, it sounded almost as if he were talking to himself.

"Sometimes we make people we love so big and perfect that it's hard to forgive them when they fall short of our vision of them."

"Rabbi," I said sharply, "do you know what my father did? I'm not talking 'falling short,' I'm talking lying and stealing and ratting on his best friend who killed himself and headlines and jail."

"I know the story, Erika. And I can only imagine your disappointment in him. It's just that the laws of society are doing such a great job of punishing him right now that if you abandon him, too . . . Well, that might be one too many doors slammed in his face."

"What would you suggest? I can't pretend my feelings toward him have changed. I can't. I wish I could . . ."

"No, no pretending. I think it's important that your dad knows how you feel. But I think that it serves neither of you for you to treat him

189

badly. Besides, I know one reason that it hurts you so is that you never imagined you were capable of acting this way toward someone you love."

I just looked at him.

"You see, the things your father needs most now—friendship, support, respect—are denied to him by the rest of the world. He can't recover them without the love of those closest to him. What he did was the act of a frightened man who was too weak to avoid the temptations around him. You certainly don't have to approve of what he did, just maybe understand what it looked like through his eyes."

His words, asking me to consider that maybe I didn't have all the information I needed to be so definite in my condemnation, reminded me of what Uncle Frank had said.

"But what about his testimony, telling on everyone? Is that right?"

"Well, I don't know all the details, but I always believe it takes more strength to tell the truth once you've done wrong than to lie. After telling the truth and dealing with the consequences, you're bigger than the wrong you committed."

I flashed on the picture of my sneaker rubbing away the evidence of Megan's tennis ball.

It was quiet for a long moment. Then he asked, "How's your brother?"

I told him about the short, cold phone calls, the canceled visits home, his high moral standards, our semi-makeup that night in my room, and Matt's refusal still to talk to Dad.

He shook his head.

"I suspect there are times we'd all like to run and hide. Matt just had the ideal opportunity. I hope he doesn't always expect a kind of perfection from himself—or anyone else." He paused for a moment, then asked, "How's your mom?"

"She's doing the best she can. I know she's really having a hard time, but she doesn't talk to me about it. She has my grandmother to confide in." I hesitated for a second. "It's hard for me to tell her how I'm feeling sometimes because I know she'd rather not hear it. She keeps lists. And one more problem added onto her list might take her over the edge."

He looked right at me with those startlingly clear eyes of his. "Just when you'd love to lean, she's not so steady. Just when you need things from her most, she has the least to give . . ."

His sympathy and concern washed over me. They gave me the courage to ask one more hard question.

"Rabbi, will I ever love my father the way I

used to?" I asked, willing to sound a little bit more like an eight-year-old than I would've liked, because the answer was so important to me.

He didn't reply right away. Then he said very softly and slowly, "Your love might not be the same as it was, but it can still be rich and strong and right. Maybe more closely based on reality. You have to ask yourself, 'Can I love my father if he's imperfect? Is it possible he's a good man who never realized how bad his actions were? Am I going to be so rigid and unforgiving that I disregard his attempts to make amends and to change?'"

My eyes filled with tears. He hadn't actually given me the answer I'd hoped for—"Of course you'll love him again, I guarantee it"— but this would do. His answer put the ball back in my court. I didn't have to be mean to Allison, have nightmares, be jealous of anyone not living in my house. I could study. I could plan to rid myself of the enormous guilt I'd been carrying around since the tennis match. I could try to let go of the anger so it didn't have to pound inside my head looking for a way out.

"Thank you so much for your time," I said, standing up kind of abruptly. I needed a tissue, three aspirin, and a long walk home to think over what he'd said.

Rabbi Beckman stood, too. He took my hand and held it between his two palms.

"Truly, Erika, it'd be my privilege to talk to you whenever you'd like."

"Next time maybe we'll cover the people in this neighborhood who live for gossip." I laughed. "Any sacred words of advice on handling them?"

"Absolutely," he answered. "Say a lot to fewer people. Say a lot less to everyone else. It won't stop it—you're right, nothing stops it—but it might slow a few tongues down to double the speed limit."

He walked me to the door. It felt perfectly natural giving him a hug.

"Whatever happens from now on is in the direction of new beginnings. This unconnected, scattered-pieces-lying-all-around feeling you have now is just temporary, I promise."

"I hope so," I said as I left. "You're really good at what you do. Thanks again. I'll be in touch."

The half-hour walk to Gram's felt like it took five minutes. When I reached the front door, I had no memory of how I got there. My mind kept going over my conversation. I couldn't put my finger on any one remark he said that made me feel better about my dad, but there was no doubt that I did. How I wished he could've done the same thing for how I felt about me.

After months of crises upon crises, life started to drag. Maybe that's just how normal life always is, but until you spend a while in bizarro land, you don't realize it. Probably Gram was right, I was impossible to make happy. First I whined about all the changes. Then when things returned to dull and boring, I wasn't one iota happier. When I thought it through, I realized the one thing that could make my life better . . . going back home.

For a while it had been bearable, not having any friends over, even having to borrow Grandma's cantaloupe nail polish because my color was home. At the beginning, when I didn't have the energy to do more than go to school, work, eat, and sleep, it was a relief to be protected from the outside world by hiding out at Gram's. I got used to not seeing Bailey that much, not experimenting with tie-dying, bleaching, or cutting up my clothes, not drinking the bottled water I lived for to maintain my skin. But now that life was settling down a little, I wanted to go back to my house.

As long as we stayed at Gram's, real life was postponed. Not that the last few months felt like a vacation, but it was make-believe life, one step removed from the real thing. I needed to blast my stereo and call Allison at one in the morning. I longed to study with my feet on my bed and my head on the floor, to leave a mess till I was ready to clean it up, to stay in the shower for a half hour if I felt like it. I wanted to invite three of my friends over to watch *Melrose*, and have a pizza delivered—without worrying about the couch or coasters or how loud we laughed. I missed choosing what I wanted to wear from my entire wardrobe, not just the practical bits and pieces I had with me. I missed my bath towel, my cereal bowl, the complete and utter privacy I found only behind the closed door of my bedroom. It was as wrong for Bailey to be taken care of by legions of helpful neighbors as it was for me to be protected from the place that brought me peace. But I knew it would not be an easy task to get back there.

I started to plan strategies—maybe telling Grandpa first and getting him to back me when the time was right—but I knew I could wait for another year and the time would never be right. I decided to drop the bomb on Friday night after dinner. We'd just finished dessert.

"I'm stuffed, Mom," said Dad, pushing back his chair from the table and wiping his mouth with a napkin. "You really outdid yourself with these cheese tarts." He used to call her Cleo, but since we moved in, he'd started calling her Mom. It was amazing that Gram, whose day could be ruined if I put a dish in the dishwasher without rinsing, could be so loving to him.

"You didn't think the crust was too doughy? This was Blossom's recipe. I like mine better," answered Gram, accepting the compliment in her typical gracious manner.

I knew I'd have to start fast if I wanted everyone's attention. In five more minutes the women would be in the kitchen, Grandpa would be dozing on the couch, Dad would be in the bathroom, and I would be hating myself for being a coward.

"Uh, before we get up, there's something I want to say," I began. I prayed that Gram wouldn't get hysterical and Dad wouldn't scowl and Mom wouldn't purse her lips.

"I've been thinking a lot lately about going back to our house." I waited a moment. No one said a word.

"Gram, you've been terrific, and for sure my clothes won't all be as clean and my suppers won't smell as good, but I really miss my room and my phone and my dog . . ."

"But, Erika, you know why we're here. I'm afraid that if we go back home, we'll be harassed all over again," said Mom. She glanced around the table, looking for support. In that instant I saw clearly that Mom was strong and in control as long as she could lean on Grandma. Those lists and her busy schedule kept her feelings and her problems at arm's distance. If we went back home, she might have to talk to Dad . . . and to me.

"I know you're afraid, Ma, but I'm not. We came here because you were trying to protect me. It was right to move out then. But it's been over four months. And it's right to move back now. We can't hide here forever."

"This is one time I'm keeping my mouth shut," said Gram, starting to stack the plates. "Whatever I say, someone will yell, so whatever you decide is fine by me."

"Erika, write down the date and the time, this is an historic occasion," said Grandpa. "Your grandmother thought first before she spoke." He smiled at Grandma and gave her a wink. Then he got up and started to clear the table. "You three sit and talk. I'll help clean up tonight."

The three of us sat quietly for a moment. Then Dad said, "I don't think the press will be much interested in me till the trial. And even then I don't think they'll bother you at home, since all the fireworks will be going off in the courtroom in Harrisburg." Because of all the headlines and rumors and Uncle Ray's suicide, a judge had ruled it would be almost impossible to hold a fair trial in New York. "Whatever you two want to do, I'll do."

Mom and I looked at each other. I knew she really didn't have a strong enough argument to fight me. That didn't mean she wouldn't try.

"You know you'll come home to an empty house after school," she started.

"You mean like I have every day since seventh grade?" I said. Then more gently, "If it's the media thing that bothers you, Mom, I'll stay at a friend's house till you come home."

"I want you to promise you'll keep the door locked any time you're by yourself, and you won't say one word to anyone." I had really caught her off guard.

"I promise," I said, trying hard not to smile.

"And if something happens, and I decide that it's better for you to come back here, I don't want any arguments." This sounded like a done deal.

"Fair enough." I smiled at them both. "It's really for the best. Going home is right for all of us," I said. "We belong in our own house. You'll see."

The kitchen door swung open, and Gram came out with an empty tray to pile all the dirty dishes on.

"So, who won?" she said, looking at each of our faces in turn. "As if I didn't know."

CHAPTER 10

New York Globe

New York's most important corruption trial in decades has been moved to Harrisburg, Pennsylvania, a place chosen because its residents are largely ignorant of the case. In the last few days, Stephen Gresham recounted how he tearfully pledged not to turn against his friend, Raymond Schuman, and how, at Schuman's suggestion, he considered suicide as their corruption scheme began to unravel. Gresham looks confused under cross-examination. There are key meetings he can't recall, giving defense counsel ammunition to damage his credibility in the eyes of the jurors. He has admitted accepting more than $150,000 in graft, which was given to him in monthly installments and which he shared fifty-fifty with Raymond Schuman.

IT WAS COMFORTING being home again, cuddling Bailey, eating potato chips in bed, smiling up at Tom Cruise. Dad was hardly around at all now. The trial was in a few weeks, and the prosecution was carefully preparing. Each night he came home with a ton of papers to read through. It looked like he was studying for finals. Mom made up her mind not to go with him to Harrisburg for the trial. She blamed not wanting to leave me alone and not being able to take the time off from work, but I was pretty sure she just couldn't handle it. Sitting in court would be friends of theirs—well, former friends—whose lives depended on what Dad said about them. He was going to be grilled by some of the best-known attorneys in New York, whose mission it would be to make him look unreliable, untrustworthy, and greedy. Given the evidence, that would not be difficult. As much as Dad wanted to have Mom with him for support, I knew he felt he didn't have the right to expect her to be there. Maybe the other guys' families were aware of what was going on from the beginning. Mom couldn't— wouldn't—pretend she stood wholeheartedly behind him. Dad wasn't to be sentenced with the others; his case would be decided separately after this trial was over. Although the verdict on his punishment was weeks away from being handed down, he had already begun serving his time.

Matt called more regularly now, at least once a week. Dad never answered the phone anymore, and Matt never asked to speak to him, so I would be the go-between, adding "color" like those guys who do the football games on TV.

"Matt wanted to know how you're holding up," I would say to Dad after I got off the phone, just slightly altering his remark, which was closer to, "Dad still alive? I don't understand how."

Or I'd say to Matt, "Dad really appreciates that you're working an extra two nights in the library to help out," when I knew that Dad did, even if he didn't say it.

If Matt wanted to know how many more days till the trial, he'd say, "How long till the freak show begins?" When he asked about what we thought Dad's sentence in jail would be, he'd say, "How much time will you and Mom be living it up as single women?" But even if his macho attitude got obnoxious, at least he called.

My friends in school were another story.

"I don't see how you and your mom aren't going with him," said Ingrid one day at lunch. "I'll bet there are reporters from all the tabloids there. They'll pay anything just for the inside scoop on how you're feeling. It's not like you even have to talk about the case or anything."

"She's right," added Laura. "Joey Buttafuoco got five hundred thousand dollars just to say how happy he was to get out of jail. You should look into it."

"Hey, cool it, girls," rebuked Allison. "Erika's dad first has to testify. He can't talk to anyone, right Erika?"

I nodded.

"This is no day at the beach for her family," she continued. "This is not *NYPD Blue*. This is not *L.A. Law*. This is reality. If they're not going to Harrisburg, it's because it's probably better for the case if they stay out of sight." She looked at the girls at the table and said condescendingly, "You want to be famous, go on *Star Search*. Meanwhile, leave Erika alone."

At that instant a flood of gratitude and relief reminded me why Allison had been my best friend since sixth grade.

Watching my father on the evening news was one of the oddest experiences I'd ever had. He looked perfectly normal, but I felt the way I did when I was about nine and accidentally caught him naked coming out of the shower. It was as if I'd trespassed on forbidden territory. The face that was as familiar to me as any in the world suddenly belonged to a stranger. I saw the familiar thinning brown hair, the white of his scalp showing through where'd he sweat and the hair clumped together. I saw the small scar that peeked out from the deepest worry line in creation across his forehead, that he got one summer in Cape Cod when we were on vacation, and the wind blew a beach chair right into his face. And along with thousands of others watching the television, I saw my father, my daddy, cry for only the second time in my life.

I was grateful that the amount of money involved (only a quarter of a million dollars) and the charges (routine white-collar stuff) were not deemed sexy enough for national exposure on *Court TV*. Three-minute snippets were painful enough; we never could have made it through hour replays and instant analyses of the proceedings. Probably if Uncle Ray had lived, he would've been charismatic enough to attract the masses. Poor Uncle Ray.

Dad stayed in Harrisburg all week, so it was just Mom and me at home watching. We sat close together, me with my math homework, she with her red pen and some article to proofread; both of us armed with something to do if it became necessary to look away. But we never could. Our eyes were locked to the screen for the three or four minutes the story appeared. Of course, not all of that time was Dad responding to reporters' questions. He shared the screen with the families of those he was incriminating, who called him everything from a liar to a lackey. On one broadcast two people were interviewed coming out of the courthouse.

"That Gresham has quite the criminal mind, if you ask me," said an elderly man who had spent most of his time in the back of courtrooms for the last eleven years since he'd retired. He admitted he'd known nothing about the case and had wandered into that particular courtroom when he saw all the photographers snapping madly at the key players as they walked in.

"To have lorded over such a complicated affair, involving so many different departments . . . No telling what he could've done if he'd gone straight."

Mom and I looked at each other. Then, at the same moment, both of us raised our eyes to the ceiling. We started to laugh, in spite of how hideous the whole thing actually was, at the absurd idea of this old guy believing that Dad was some kind of brilliant gangster.

The other person interviewed was the

brother of one of the men Dad was implicating in the case.

"He was nothing but Schuman's gofer. This guy never had an original thought in his life. He's just become real creative 'cause his lawyer told him the easiest way to save himself is to spread his slime on anyone he ever dealt with. How can you believe a word he says?"

The trial was even covered in Connecticut. Greg understood for the first time what the whole scandal was about.

"I always knew what your dad did was wrong, Erika, but the way they keep asking him the same questions, over and over, is a bit cruel and unusual if you ask me," he said at the end of the first week of testimony.

"That's because each of the people he's incriminating has his own lawyer," I said wearily. "If one of them was my dad, I'd want his lawyer to ask them, too."

"He has your eyes."

"What?"

"Your father. He has the same color blue eyes as you do. I know it's off the topic, but I watch the news just to see his—your—eyes. Does that sound lame?"

I laughed. "There's nothing I'd rather talk about but things off the topic, and if you want to see eyes that look like mine so badly that you sit through the news, I'm flattered."

"Thirty more days and they'll look back at me," Greg said. "I can't wait."

My belly flopped. He was still counting the days. Would he be as eager to see me if he knew what else my dad and I shared—the secret of how I really won the tennis championship?

Dad was on the stand for a week and a half. At night he went back to his hotel room alone. Everyone else involved, according to Dad, spent quiet time with their families. He'd read some material the district attorney had prepared for him, then he'd call us. I'd answer the phone and speak to him as if he were out of town on a business trip. I never told him I watched him on TV, knowing there was nothing I could share with him that could possibly make him feel better. When I asked him how his day went, he'd say, "I've had better," or "The best thing about it is that it's over." Then I'd say that I had to get off the phone to get my clothes out or study for a test or call Allison. He probably knew it wasn't the truth, but it was easier for both of us this way. I'd say, "Hold on for Mom," as if she wasn't one inch away from me, then I'd go into the kitchen and let them talk in private.

As bad as I knew Mom felt about him being alone, I knew she'd never be able to sit in that courtroom and listen. Dad had protected her once by not telling her the gory details; this time she was protecting herself. I overheard her saying very little, those nights on the phone. As I left the room I'd watch her take the same position, lying across the couch with her eyes closed, one arm cupped over her forehead, squeezing her temples as she made little, one-syllable sounds—"Uh-huh," "Wow," "No." The calls lasted about a half hour. Then she'd just lie there, the phone on her stomach, just staring at the ceiling for another fifteen minutes. I'd hear a loud sigh, and she'd dial Grandma for a two-minute rehashing of the day.

I pretended I was busy finishing my home-work at the kitchen table. Actually half my mind did the work due the next day; the other half reran the pictures on the TV screen. I never cried, not once during those two weeks. What I was feeling wasn't sharp and cutting enough for tears. What I was feeling was that old friend, heavy, almost overwhelming sad-ness, devoid of any passion or energy.

"How's he doing?" I asked my mother when she peeked her head into the kitchen on her way up to bed.

"He's hanging in there," she answered, blowing me a kiss as she dragged herself up the stairs.

I'd follow her and turn out the lights soon after and think about what monumental courage it sometimes takes to simply hang in there. And how sometimes it was almost heroic just to be able to fall asleep at the end of the day.

I woke up on my seventeenth birthday wishing I could postpone it for a day when I'd be more in the mood. At least it was a Friday. Mom invited Grandma and Grandpa over for dinner. That assured a homemade marble cake for dessert, no small bonus.

I got to school and Allison, Laura, and Ingrid decorated my locker with balloons, a Brad Pitt poster, and some crepe paper streamers. At lunch they all sang "Happy Birthday" and gave me a fifty-dollar gift certificate to Record World. After months of feeling isolated I was surprised to find myself so choked up.

"Thanks, guys," I said. "I can't believe you remembered."

"We didn't," said Laura. "Allison did."

I looked at Allison and saw her smiling.

"Wow, I never saw anybody cry over a completely impersonal gift certificate before," said Ingrid. "Imagine if we'd bought her the car we were thinking about."

Everyone laughed.

"I really appreciate your patience, guys. I know I've been pretty drippy lately," I said. "Once my father finishes testifying and finds out what his punishment is, then I'll rejoin the land of the living, I promise."

They were all very quiet. Then Laura said, "I don't think I'd have been able to handle all this as well as you, Erika. You've been so brave."

"Me, too," said Ingrid. "I would've been crying and complaining every day. I think you're doing amazing."

Amazing. They should only know.

"Uh, we want to apologize, if we, uh, got a little carried away with the hype of the whole thing," Laura said. She looked at me for permission to go on. "I don't think *we* handled this whole thing too well . . . Because you always acted like you were OK, a little embarrassed maybe, but basically OK, I guess we didn't realize that making light of what your dad did might not have been what you wanted to hear. We didn't know what to say. If we acted dumb, we're sorry . . ."

All three heads nodded in agreement.

"I'm partly to blame for that," I said. "You tried to make me feel better by saying you thought what he did wasn't so terrible. But for me and my mom it really was. I realize now that you couldn't possibly have known how I felt. I never told you."

We all just sat there and grinned.

"Thanks for staying with me, guys. I almost forgot how good it feels to have friends." The bell rang, and we got up from the cafeteria table.

As we moved toward the door, we came face to face with Mr. DaMaio and Stacey.

"Your father looks good on TV," she said in a stupid attempt at conversation. "I think he's getting his point across very well."

"You think so?" I said.

"Yeah. What do you think, Mr. DaMaio?" She looked at him with that big-eyed, phony smile. "Don't you think Mr. Gresham's doing a good job in court?"

I don't know who wanted to strangle her more, Mr. DaMaio or me.

"I haven't forgotten about getting back to you, Mr. DaMaio," I blurted out. "I'm just not sure yet. I'll get in to see you next week—I promise."

"Sure about what?" Stacey's eyes narrowed. "Playing next year? You said you weren't. I specifically asked you a few weeks ago, and you said you weren't."

Poor Stacey. She'd probably already dusted off the place over her fireplace for her Most

Outstanding Senior Award. It would almost be worth playing again just to see her face.

"You're full of questions today, aren't you, Stacey?" said Mr. DaMaio. "I don't want to be rude, but my impressions of Mr. Gresham's behavior on TV and the details of my conversation with Erika are none of your concern." He did a perfect imitation of her smile and gave it right back to her.

"I must be going," he said, pulling away from us. "I'll look forward to hearing from you soon," he whispered to me as he passed by.

We left Stacey standing there and went to our next class.

That night rounded out the surprising sweetness of the day. UPS brought a long, narrow box with a dozen long-stemmed chocolate roses. The card said,

> *Sweet and familiar,*
> *but with a delicious twist.*
> *These roses and you . . .*
> *Happy Birthday,*
>
> > *Greg*

Grandma and Grandpa bought me a stereo to replace the one taken away. "We said to the man, 'Just give us the best one you got,' right, Willard?" said Gram, motioning to Grandpa to second their generosity. "See, we did good," she continued, carefully watching my face.

Aunt Shirley had come for dinner also. She bought me beautiful stationery with my name embossed on it.

"I figured you're going away this summer, you could use some nice stationery," she said.

"Oh, Aunt Shirley, it's perfect. I promise to write you first."

"Never mind writing me. I'm not fussy about things like that," she said, looking pointedly at her sister. "Just enjoy, that's all."

The phone rang.

"Erika, it's your brother," yelled Gram from the kitchen. "The one who forgets for months at a time he has grandparents."

"Oh, *that* brother," I said, getting up from the table to take the phone.

Everyone chuckled as I closed the door behind me and sat down to talk to Matt.

"Happy birthday, little sister," he said. "Sorry I can't be there with you."

"That's OK," I said. "I'm just glad you called."

"Did you get my card?"

"No, when did you mail it?" A card and a call. Amazing.

"Two days ago," he said. "I'm going to spoil the surprise if I tell you, but I don't care. In the card are two tickets to *Les Miserables* for the end of August when you get back from camp. I knew you wanted to see it, and I figured the two of us could use a night out together. So just keep them in a safe place, OK?"

This was the best gift yet. "Oh, Matt, that'll be great. Thank you."

"No, Erika, thank *you*," he said in a serious tone, "for pulling my load this year." If I didn't know better, I would swear he sounded choked up.

It was like one of those sixty-second Kodak commercials that get you all teary because they sentimentalize the best of what a family can be.

"I love you, too," I said to Matt. "You want to talk to Mom?" I added quickly, feeling a lump starting to grow in my throat.

"Uh-huh." He paused. "Is Dad home?"

This was the first time all year he even asked.

"No, he's still in Harrisburg. He finished testifying today, and he's going to stay there till they decide on a sentence for him." I was pleased that he asked. I wondered, if I had said Dad was home, whether he would've spoken to him.

I helped Mom clean up when everyone left.

"I can't believe how much better this birth-

day turned out than I thought it would,"
I said.

"Good, I'm glad," she said. "I was a bit
shaky about it myself. It felt strange not having
your father here."

It would have felt stranger for me, I
thought, if he'd been home.

"By the way," Mom continued, "Dad left
you a birthday card before he left. It's behind
the toaster oven. Don't be angry with him for
not calling. He's just hanging by a thread till
the sentencing, and I think he thought he'd
bring you down if he called."

I didn't expect to hear from him. And I was
glad he didn't call. I reached for his card and
kissed her good night.

Then I called to Bailey to come up to my
room. Whatever the card said, I needed her
moral support. She came in an instant, and we
both lay down across the bed. I ripped open the
envelope. Instead of a card was a note written
on a small piece of paper ripped out of the back
of his Filofax.

Dear Erika,
    Pardon the inappropriate stationery
but it's all I have handy. I want you to
know how proud I am of you. I don't think

I could get through this if I didn't draw strength from your mother and you, and even your stubborn brother these past six months.

Happy, happy birthday, my sweet baby. You might've chosen a smarter father, but you could never have found one who loves you more.

Love,
Daddy

I read it over three times. I felt something, but I wasn't sure what. Maybe it was the stirrings of forgiveness, or at least a lifting of the terrible heaviness that accompanied every thought of him. Or maybe it was just pity.

The next week Dad was given an eighteen-month jail sentence at a minimum security prison in Massachusetts. The newspapers said that despite his extensive cooperation with the government, he had committed "a massive crime of a very, very serious nature." Having it down in black and white—the day he'd be leaving, where he'd be going, the length of time he'd be spending in jail—brought us one step closer to the end of the nightmare.

CHAPTER 11

New York Daily Mirror

Stephen Gresham was sentenced to eigh-teen months in prison and three years proba-tion for his participation in New York State's Education Department corruption scandal. He is scheduled to surrender July 30 and is expected to serve his time at the federal prison in Ellenville, Massachusetts. Despite the prosecutor's repeated enthusias-tic praise of Mr. Gresham's "extraordinary cooperation," Judge Peller said, "I cannot let people out there believe they can commit any crime they want to commit, and if they cooperate with the government, they will get a free ride."

IF ANYONE would've told me that when I found out my father was going to jail for eigh-teen months I would feel more relief than I did sadness or shame, I'd have said they were out of their mind. But relief was overwhelmingly my emotion of choice that day. Sentencing meant the public part of Dad's role in the scandal would be over.

For once Dad's timing was impeccable. School ended on Wednesday, he was sentenced on Friday, and I was leaving for camp on Saturday. I didn't have to face Mr. Datz, who I'm sure would've put Dad away for twenty years. Or the dirtbags, who probably wanted my autograph now that my father was a convicted felon, or Stacey, whose smirk would be barely hidden underneath her pitying eyes and solicitous words.

I watched the news that night with Mom as she helped me stuff too many pillows, blankets, and sheets into my duffel bag. The screen showed a drawing of Dad that one of those court artists did. It was a sketch of him sitting with his hands folded in front of him, his head slightly bowed, and a slight frown on his face.

"Gresham rose only briefly to speak on his own behalf," said the announcer, "and, in a voice choked with emotion, offered an apology for his crimes to the public, his family, and friends. 'I understand my words can't take away the pain and suffering I've caused,' he said. 'I can only promise to spend the rest of my life trying to earn back the respect I've lost.' "

Mom and I watched in silence.

"How far is Ellenville?" I asked, as matter-of-factly as if I were asking what time the bus was leaving the next day.

"I'm not really sure," she answered. "I think about six hours."

"That's not bad," I said, putting my finger in the center of the knot Mom was tying to close the duffel. "We could do that on a week-end easy."

"Yeah, easy," she replied, not looking at me.

"And I'll be driving soon, won't that be fun?" I said. "It won't be bad if we have two drivers."

"No," Mom said. "It won't be bad. In fact, compared to the rest of this year, it'll be a piece of cake."

It wasn't until I went to sleep that night that I realized we hadn't mentioned one word about the length of the sentence, Dad's apology, or the whole idea of us living without him for a year and a half. Like I said, how you feel when something like this happens and how you think you're going to feel are two different things.

The person I did get to speak to before school ended was Mr. DaMaio. I postponed my meeting with him till the last day of school.

And still I wasn't sure of what I was going to say until I knocked on his door.

"You can come in," he yelled, "only if you're not bringing me any more problems."

His office was a mess. Dozens of lists, stray pieces of equipment from every sport from lacrosse to softball, half-empty cartons, and four mugs with remnants of unrecognizable liquids littered every square inch of space.

"I'm donating those cups to science, what do you think?" he said, as if he were expecting me to pop through the door at exactly that moment.

"Smart idea," I went along. "There might be a possible cure for scurvy lurking in those mugs."

"Sit down . . . if you can find a chair," he said as he continued to pack up for summer vacation.

"No, that's OK, I'd rather stand," I replied. "I know you're busy so I'll make it fast . . ."

Mr. DaMaio stopped what he was doing, leaned back against the wall, folded his arms, and said, "Take your time and make it right."

I took a deep breath and started.

"You were right. The reasons I gave you for not wanting to play tennis were just excuses. I didn't want to play because my father loved that I played. As much as I enjoy it, he enjoys it more. And the last thing I wanted to do is do anything that would bring him pleasure."

Mr. DaMaio nodded.

"I knew if I quit he would feel bad. It was the one thing I could do without flunking out of school that would get his attention. It was the easiest way I could think of to hurt him. So I decided to quit."

I stopped.

"And now?" Mr. DaMaio said impatiently, motioning with his hand that I should continue.

"And now I decided that was stupid," I finished.

Confessing to being stupid was far easier than confessing the truth about how I won my last match. I knew that my punishment, a life sentence of keeping it a secret, would cure me of the temptation of ever doing anything like that again.

Mr. DaMaio nodded. "Bravo. The old cutting-off-your-nose-to-spite-your-face move exposed as garbage once again. Good for you, Erika."

I smiled weakly. "I realized that taking away one of the things that makes me feel good about myself is not the way to go. I can't make my father's troubles be my reason for doing or not doing anything." As soon as the words came out of my mouth, I knew they were true. I stood up taller. On a conscious level I hadn't had a clue to how I was going to explain how I felt or why I decided to play again. Thank God for my hardworking unconscious.

"I'm sure he'd be the first to agree," Mr. Da-Maio said, turning serious.

"Well, I'm playing because I'm doing what's best for me. And that means letting go of whether it pleases him or not."

"OK, OK—take it easy. You win. Everyone wins . . . As long as you're still on the team, I'm happy. You made the right decision, Erika, regardless of whether or not I agree with your reasoning."

"Thanks, Mr. DaMaio, for handling me exactly right. And for not falling for my 'poor me' routine."

"We coaches have Gatorade running through our veins," he said as he flexed his biceps. He winked and added, "Now go have the best summer of your life, and come back to me ready to work your butt off."

"I will," I smiled as I walked to the door. "You're a great coach."

"Aach," he said, waving me away and turning his attention back to the chaos in front of him. "So great I'll be here till September trying to clean up this place."

The last day of school is usually one of the highlights of my year. Endless school replaced by endless summer. I decided to walk home the long way and sit by the pond for a while. I needed to sort out why I felt so lousy on such a glorious day.

This year ending should've felt even more spectacular than usual. Ask anyone, my life was improving every day. After surviving months of living without my room, without real friends, without my brother, things were returning to normal. Dad was finally almost out of the limelight. I could count the time till I'd see Greg in mere hours. Next year I'd be a senior. If these weren't flashes of that proverbial light at the end of the tunnel, I don't know what would be. And yet I felt none of the relief you would expect to feel when everything is finally going your way.

I reached the pond and was grateful to find it deserted. I sat down on a bench and searched my backpack for remnants of food to feed the ducks. As I threw a few jelly beans into the water and watched how they fought over them, the reason for my misery became clear.

It was shame that gnawed away at every

happy moment. As time went on, I was becoming more uncomfortable with my cheating—and the hidden price of getting away with it—than I was with what my father did. *His* guilt wasn't growing inside anymore. I had watched as sunlight and public scrutiny slowly melted it down. His wounds were healing; mine were still festering. He was balancing his moral account; I was way short on my ethics deposits.

Suddenly I knew that I'd never be able to pick up a tennis racket and be proud of my performance until I unburdened myself. I could go on and win the U.S. Open and still feel like a phony and a fraud inside.

I scrounged around the bottom of my bag and came up with some lint-covered raisins to feed my honking friends. OK, so now what? If I tell, what's going to happen to me? Ridiculously, the face of the least important person in my life—a cackling Stacey—loomed large to taunt me. Then I thought of Grandpa and Matt. It was eighty degrees, but I shuddered imagining their disappointment.

I thought about when Allison's dad hurt his elbow playing basketball. It wasn't broken . . . He just couldn't straighten it out all the way. He had a choice. He could go through his life with one and a half normal arms or he could have surgery. If they operated, they'd have to break his arm in order to fix it. He decided that surgery and physical therapy afterward were too big a price to pay. So for years now he'd had limited use of his right arm.

I couldn't settle for limited use of my self-esteem. I had to confess that I cheated at the tennis match. That excruciating shame would be my operation. The weeks, maybe months after I told, till I earned their trust back, that would be my physical therapy. Then I'd be healed. It was risky, but the alternative, living "safe" and feeling miserable, made my decision clear.

OK, who do I tell first? Oh God, Greg. Then Mom. Then Allison. Then Mr. DaMaio. I took a deep breath. For the first time all day I felt how good the warm sun felt.

"Sorry, guys, I don't have anything else to feed you," I said to the ducks patiently awaiting more snacks. "I'm leaving early tomorrow morning. Do you think it's all right if I wait till I get back from camp to tell everyone other than Greg? He'll be the hardest one to be honest with—the riskiest choice to tell first. Wish me luck." I smiled as they squawked their reply.

"I'll take that as a show of support," I said as I gathered my things and headed home. It was amazing how much lighter I felt just resolving to tell the truth. If I could begin to forgive myself, I had to have faith that those who care about me would do the same.

Ah, finally. The liberating, freedom-fulfilling, full-of-promise last day of school.

My bus pulled up to camp ten minutes before Greg's did, giving me a chance to position myself behind a pile of duffel bags being unloaded from underneath the bus. From there I could watch out for him before he saw me. I was really nervous. What if we just clicked long-distance? What if when we were together it was just the same good-old-chums feeling we'd shared for years? I crouched down lower and watched as his bus came to a stop. The doors opened. He was wearing gray Umbro soccer shorts with black spandex underneath and a black tank top that showed off his strong arms. His hair was different from last summer, still black and curly but now shorter in the front and real long in the back. As he helped some of the younger kids off the bus, I saw his eyes searching around the parking lot. I hoped he was looking for me.

What am I doing, playing ridiculous games? I thought to myself as I stood up and started toward him. Then he saw me. The sudden jolt in the pit of my belly assured me we were no longer just pals.

"Hey, we made it," Greg said with a smile as we fell into a comfortable hug. There was no mistaking how glad he was to see me.

"Yep, we did," I answered. "You look great. Since when did you become such a cool dresser?"

"Since there was a reason to bother," he said, looking at me in a way that made me conscious of how fast my heart was pounding and how damp and sweaty my palms were.

I looked right into his eyes and smiled.

"I'm really happy to see you," I said, loving how nice it felt to say what I was really thinking to a boy.

"Me, too," Greg answered. "Listen, I have to take these little creatures to their bunks and help them unpack. What about meeting me at the soccer field in an hour? It's their rest period, and we can sneak a few minutes before activities start."

"Great idea," I said. "I'll see you at two."

I had to force myself to turn and walk back to where my bus was still unloading. When I got there, I looked toward Greg's bus to catch another glimpse of him. There he was, hands on his hips, just looking right back at me. I think we both blushed, then we laughed. He gave me a thumbs-up sign. It was going to be OK. I couldn't remember when I had felt so alive and totally happy.

He was waiting for me at the far end of the field. There were kids to my left making their way down to the lake and buses still unloading to my right, but I was scarcely aware of them. All of my attention was focused on Greg. He waved, and my heart moved inside me. There'd be no more fighting each day to keep old memories vivid. Finally the time was here to create new ones.

He had gathered some wildflowers and awkwardly handed them to me. I smiled. As I took them from him and raised them to my nose, I was conscious only of his glance passing over my eyes, my cheeks, my mouth.

"So, how've you been?" I said ridiculously.

"Oh, fine," he answered with a silly grin.

"You're smiling."

"I'm happy," he said simply, letting the smile go on. He came closer and put his arms around me.

"Oh, Erika," he said, rubbing his chin against the top of my head.

I could feel him still smiling. Then he took a small step back and gently took off my glasses. "You remember what I look like, don't you?" he said softly.

He bent over and kissed my eyelids, then the tip of my nose. And then there was nothing in the world but Greg and the sound of his heart thudding against me.

"Whoa," I said at last, breaking away. We smiled at each other a bit sheepishly and waited for the world to come back into focus.

We both spoke at the same moment. I said, "That was worth waiting for." He said, "That was even better than I imagined." Then we both laughed.

He sat down on a big rock near the net. He reached out and pulled me over to his lap. I could feel the muscles of his legs supporting me, his arms around me, the smell of freshly cut grass surrounding us. He held my head against his neck and whispered, "I've missed you so much."

I closed my eyes and let my whole body relax.

We sat there, just holding on to each other without speaking, for a long while. Months' worth of doubt and fear broke up all at once within me.

I thought about how sweet the moment was. I always dreamed of being dazzled by a boy's looks, or being overwhelmed by his mystery or genius or badness. But to fall for someone even my grandmother would approve of was too good to be true.

"Oh, Greg," I said, my voice cracking with emotion, "you're exactly what I needed." I cleared my throat, suddenly aware that people might be watching and a dozen eight-year-old girls would be missing me by now.

"To be continued," he said, giving my hand a final squeeze before turning toward boys' camp.

"To be continued," I repeated, smiling back at him as I ran up the hill to my bunk.

One day ran into another in the slow, unchanging pace of summer at camp. We arranged to have the same day off and the same OD. The on duty shift, where you patrol the campgrounds at night, checking on little kids who lived to torture you, was a least-favorite activity for most counselors. But Greg and I didn't mind. After the kids fell asleep, we'd sit for hours under the stars, rocking in a hammock on the porch, and talk. I told him the whole story of what happened, starting with the car ride to Edgemont six months ago. For the first time I talked not only about what happened but how I felt about what happened. He didn't say much, but the way he held me as he listened was enough. I never imagined you could give—and receive—so much comfort without saying a word.

We spent our days off taking a bus into town, going to a movie, and eating huge hoagies filled with salami, ham, provolone, onions, lettuce, and tomatoes. Before, I had always looked at those huge heroes with disgust. Now, with Greg, they were the best thing I'd ever tasted. We listened to the radio, chose the songs whose melodies we'd use for this year's color-war tunes, and just appreciated how lucky we were.

Then one night as we were walking back to our bunks, I knew the time had come to tell him about the tennis tournament. "Come sit down for a second," I said, motioning to the swing on the front porch of my bunk. "I have to talk to you."

Greg plopped down next to me. "That sounds ominous. Is anything wrong?" The concern in his voice, always soothing and welcome before, now made what I had to say even harder.

I drew my knees up under my chin and clasped my arms tightly around them. "Remember this winter, when I won the tennis tournament?" I took a deep breath. "Well . . . I cheated. I called a ball out that was really in.

And we won because I lied." I laid my face against my knees, away from Greg. The night, which had been so warm and comfortable just minutes ago, seemed dark and silent.

"Why? Why was it so important that you win that match?" Greg asked quietly.

"It wasn't. I did it to punish my father. He was watching, and I knew it would kill him to see me do something so wrong." I laughed bitterly and continued, "Instead it just gave me another reason to blame him for ruining my life."

"To get revenge on your dad, you won the match illegally?" Greg shook his head. "Wow. Did he say anything to you?"

"How could he? What could he say— 'That's not the way I brought you up? Don't ever do it again?' "

I turned to steal a look at Greg's face, but he was staring straight ahead. "I'm sorry I've disappointed you. The closer we've gotten, the harder it's been keeping this from you." I straightened my legs and started to get up. "You don't have to say anything . . . I don't expect you to . . ."

"Don't go in," interrupted Greg.

"You're the first person who knows, the one I was most afraid of telling." My voice continued on its own, shrill and panicky. "It was such a risk . . . but if I didn't tell you soon, I was afraid I might never. And then I wouldn't be accepting responsibility . . . and it would always be between us."

"It's OK, Erika, it's OK," Greg said quietly. "You're not the only one in the world who's ever felt guilt." He paused. "If you trust me enough to confess something you're so ashamed of, I can't sit here and pretend I don't know what that feels like."

I stared at him.

"Last November, I took a Shakespeare paper my sister had written three years ago in freshman English and handed it in as mine. I knew she'd never let me use it, so I went to Kinkos, made a copy, and returned the original without her ever knowing."

The air was very still.

Of all the possible ways I'd pictured Greg might respond, I'd never guessed he'd have a secret burden of his own to reveal.

"I didn't even retype it," he said, shaking his head.

"What happened?"

"What do you think?" he said with a thin smile. "I was the only one in the junior class to get an A. I had to read it out loud in front of everyone. I was in a panic for weeks that my parents would say something—brag about my grade to my sister. Never in my wildest dreams did I imagine it could feel so horrible to get away with cheating." He looked up at the sky. "My friends all suspected something, but I never told anyone. Till now."

A flood of relief quickened my heartbeat.

My shoulders, which had been scrunched up to my ears, relaxed. I reached for his hand.

"I never thought of spilling one's guts as a communal activity," I said.

Then Greg said the best thing he could have: "If there was ever a doubt that we are right for each other, it's erased forever. The worst part is over. Now all we have to do is stay close to make sure neither of us is ever that stupid again."

I spoke to my mother on Sundays, and we chatted superficially about our days. She casually mentioned Dad would be leaving for Ellenville in two weeks.

"Is there anything you want me to bring up when we come?" she asked on the Sunday before visiting day.

Is there some way you could leave Dad home? I silently asked her. "No, not really," is what I said loud enough for her to hear.

"You don't want Doritos or chocolate chip cookies or bubble gum?" she asked.

"No. Really, Mom, this summer I don't need that stuff. My complexion will thank you. The camp scale will be grateful. And I won't get up Monday morning hating myself."

"OK, honey. Whatever you say. We should be up by eleven. I'll be the one with the rose in my teeth."

"And I'll be the one with the pig tattoo on my left breast and the diamond stud in my right nostril."

We both laughed and hung up. I was happy she was coming. I wanted to introduce her to my girls, my friends, and especially to Greg. But Dad, that was a different story. No one at camp said a word about my father. I wasn't sure if that was because they had good manners, or it just wasn't important to them, or they never really knew. Whatever the reason, I was grateful. The days went by, and I hardly thought about him. And when I did, it was in a detached kind of way, like he was a neighbor or a friend of the family. I'd think, Is he counting the days? Is he scared? Or is he just resigned to getting it over with? The night before visiting day Greg and I took a walk in the woods behind the dining hall.

"I wish he wasn't coming tomorrow," I said, kicking a pebble into the water. "Do I sound like a terrible person?"

"No," Greg answered seriously. "You sound like you have to do something you're not looking forward to, like going to the dentist or taking a chem test. There'd be something wrong with you if you looked forward to saying goodbye to your father for almost two years."

We walked on. "That's not it. You're giving me too much credit. I just don't want to spoil the best summer of my life by having to deal with his mess again, that's all. I don't know what to say to him."

"How could you? You were never in this position before. Remember, it's not a stranger, it's your dad. You'll say the right thing."

I wanted to tell him that I knew the right thing to say, I just didn't feel like saying it. How could I say the sweet, kind things like, "I'm going to miss you, I'll come visit, I'll write," when I'd never said the unkind things that were on the tip of my tongue for months. "Why were you so greedy? How could you be so selfish? How come you never apologized to me for ruining my life?" I went to sleep early, praying the night would last a month so I wouldn't have to face the next day.

CHAPTER 12

When Mom says 11:00, she doesn't mean 11:05. I saw her and Dad dragging a huge picnic basket and some blankets up the hill from the parking area. I ran to help them, grateful my mind had no more time to think.

"You look gorgeous," said Mom, giving me a hug, "tan and strong and beautiful." She looked so relieved, it never entered my mind till that second she might've been worried about how I'd adjust to being away from home this particular summer.

"It's because she's happy. Look at her, relaxed and happy." Dad, on the other hand, looked pale and tired, but his face was without that tight, strained look that had been there since Christmas. "OK, where is he?" he joked, just the way he normally would. The difference was he stood back, carefully not coming close enough for a hug.

"I'll introduce you in a minute," I said with

a grin. I was determined to maintain a smiley face all afternoon. I'd figured out my best bet was to keep up the small talk and avoid being alone with either of them. I was successful for hours. I made them sit through my bunk's rendition of *Annie*, then dragged them down to the waterfront to meet Greg.

He was busy signing out water skis and boats to the families who wanted to take full advantage of their one day together in the country. As soon as he saw us, though, he handed the sheet to his assistant and sat with us on the grass.

I could see he was nervous at first, but he was so charming that no one else would ever know. Mom began the interrogation with some question about exactly what his duties running the waterfront were. By the time he finished answering, there was no doubt she'd be telling Grandma what a "caring, responsible young man Erika's Gregory is." Dad took the casual approach, asking what was his favorite baseball team. When he found out it was his very own Mets, both of them were off and running, slipping into the easy jock language of sports. We stayed for a while, then I left Mom and Dad on their own to give me a chance to meet the parents of my campers. I lingered longer than

I had to, to avoid facing the confrontation I knew was inevitable.

Finally it was almost four o'clock. There was only a half hour left before I had to be back at the bunks to distract my little campers from missing their parents. It was so easy solving the problems of eight-year-olds. The world could be coming to an end one minute, but promise them a pizza at midnight, and all's well with the universe. Mom glanced at her watch, sighed one of her let's-get-the-show-on-the-road sighs, and began packing up the leftovers from lunch. I got up to shake out the blanket.

"Let me give you a hand with that," my father offered. He held open a huge black plastic trash bag for me to dump the day's remnants in. My mom shoved everything that needed to go home in a big straw bag they had bought years ago on a vacation in Mexico.

"I'm going to bring this to the car," she said. "You two could probably use a few minutes alone. Why don't you meet me in the parking lot when you're done."

Nice going, Mom, I thought. The day had been civil and pleasant up to that point, and I had no desire to be alone with my father. How was I supposed to say good-bye? "Hope time passes by fast in the slammer? Here's wishing it's not as horrible, lonely, frightening, boring, and frustrating as we both think it will be." Long good-byes are like pulling off a Band-Aid slowly. You think it's going to be easier, but it only prolongs the hurting.

"Come on," said my father, "let's find a place to toss this." For months I had wanted nothing more than for him to leave my life in peace. He and his mistakes had been with me all the time. I looked forward to days of not hearing about him, being embarrassed by him, having pity on him. I was exhausted from hating him. But as I walked alongside him, I tried hard not to picture him in a cell, taking communal showers, growing old.

We arrived at the far end of the deserted tennis courts and threw the trash in a huge bin. Muted squeals of little girls being tickled and little boys being chased drifted over our way. Our silence was getting on my nerves.

"Are you scared?" I was surprised to hear myself ask. My dad reached for my hand. It was the first time we had touched in a long time. He slowly, purposefully interlaced his fingers with mine and started to walk toward the lake. My heart started to beat faster. I really wasn't ready for a dramatic parting-is-such-sweet-sorrow scene. I wished we were headed back to Mom.

"Of prison, sure, but I'll survive," he answered. "There are things I fear worse than going to jail."

"Like what?" I asked, not able, on that gorgeous sunny afternoon, to think of anything more horrible than being locked up.

"Like losing you."

I didn't answer. So many months and he never once showed me he was worried about how I felt.

"Like coming back in a year and a half and finding a young woman who has filled in my space in her life so that I'm no longer necessary."

Oh, Daddy, don't make me feel guilty for not promising that things will be the same as they were. Why did you have to be so weak? Why did you have to tell on Uncle Ray? The words were loud inside my head. I knew that if I said anything, my voice would crack, and I was determined that I would handle this without crying.

We stopped in front of a large oak tree overlooking the water. Dad sat down on the grass, his back leaning up against the trunk. He motioned for me to do the same. If we had to talk, at least it was easier not facing him.

241

"I know you see me as cowardly," he began, "but facing the music is never the easy way out. Look at Uncle Ray. He masterminded a different ending."

It was the first time since the suicide that he'd mentioned Uncle Ray's name.

"Before the story broke in the press, the day after we came back from Edgemont at Christmastime, Ray begged me to run away with him. He had worked out all the details—phony passports, transfer of money, safe passage for both of us to escape from prosecution."

"Why didn't you go?"

"I couldn't leave you and Matt and Mom to clean up my mess!" he said emphatically. "When I refused, he begged me to commit suicide with him. When I said no to that, he promised that somehow we'd get through this together, that I shouldn't worry, he'd tell the truth about how this whole operation was in the works long before I started to work at the State Education Department." He sighed. "But he just couldn't face it. He couldn't bear being exposed."

"So it wasn't your testimony that killed him?"

"No, Erika. He committed suicide because of his own weakness, not mine."

It was hard for me to picture Uncle Ray as

weak. I had never thought of my father's testifying as the brave thing to do.

"But why, Daddy? We didn't need the money. Why did you take such a big risk for nothing?" I finally asked him the question that had been gnawing at me for a year.

"The money was the smallest part of it. After Uncle Ray put himself out on a limb to get me this job when I went bankrupt, I felt I owed him. It wasn't till months later that I realized that part of my job was to be a glorified middleman between power brokers. I won't lie to you—part of me loved being in the center of things, being respected, having people want to be my friend. But when I started getting uncomfortable, I should have left. I was stupid—and scared. And you know how persuasive Uncle Ray could be . . ."

I could tell he was forcing himself to continue.

"The money was never important. I hated it. I spent it the minute I got it. If I would've saved to buy anything of value, it would've always been a reminder of where it came from. Some nights, coming home from the city through the Midtown Tunnel, I used to scream at the top of my lungs inside the car with the windows closed. I yelled and cried and screamed till I was exhausted. I was trapped. I couldn't talk to Mommy. I was in too far to back out. And I hated myself so. I think that was the worst time of all."

It had never entered my mind that he might have suffered before he was found out, more than he did from seeing lies in the newspaper destroying his reputation forever, from seeing his best friend die. More than being humiliated for weeks on trial. My eyes started to sting, but I didn't look at him.

"I wanted to die a thousand times through this past year. If I was handling my day OK, I couldn't bear the thought of how much harder I made yours. I tried to convince myself I was teaching you valuable life lessons. That by witnessing what happens when you lose your integrity, when you're no longer your own person, when you give up having control over your own destiny—Oh God, I'm so sorry, Erika."

I turned around to check out the pain on his face. In my dreams I hadn't counted on the pain being contagious.

"Dad," I suddenly blurted, "there's something I have to explain to you. You have a right to know why I did what I did . . . at the tennis match."

"I know, Erika, I know," he said softly.

"It wasn't planned or anything," I began in a rush. "I don't want you to think I wanted to win so badly that I'd lie like that . . . That's not why I cheated." I felt my heart beating in my throat. "It never would've happened if you hadn't shown up."

My dad didn't say a word.

"When I saw you standing there on the sidelines, all I could think about was getting back at you for embarrassing me by coming to the game. I was sure everyone was talking about me—and it was all your fault."

I took a deep breath and forced myself to continue.

"Then that last ball landed so close to the line . . . I knew no one could know for sure whether it was in or out—except you."

My voice broke. "I was sorry ten seconds after I did it. It'll never happen again, I promise. I told Greg last week. And as soon as I get home, I'm going to tell Mom and Mr. DaMaio and Allison. It's too hard keeping it in." I stuck my hand in my shorts and found an old tissue. "Once they know, I can deal with it and then put it behind me." I blew my nose loudly. Dad nodded and gave me a small smile. There was a soft breeze, and we sat silently for a while.

I lay my head back on his chest and closed my eyes. Strange pictures flashed before them. Dad warming up Mom's car ten minutes before she had to leave for work each winter morning

'cause she hated getting into a freezing car.
Dad adding an orange to my lunch, carefully
peeled and wrapped in tinfoil, whenever I had
a cold.

"What are you going to do there all day?
I mean, what kinds of things to keep yourself
busy?" I asked.

"I don't really know. They'll give me a job
I'm sure I can handle. And I'll have a chance
for the first time in years to work on this poor
abused body of mine. Take a good look at it
now. I'm planning to leave half of it behind."

I wondered what he'd look like thin and fit.

"It'll be a relief to get this over with," he
continued. "I just want to concentrate on a
time when I can put all of this behind us and
start planning our future."

"Our future." The words echoed in my
mind. I had given up on even thinking of "us"
having a future. I wanted to say, I recognize
you in there, Daddy, buried under the headlines. I'm going to try to concentrate on that
part. I'm going to think about how, no matter
how stupid your mistakes, you've been punished and you've suffered. And how you've
never blamed anyone but yourself. I hope all
that stuff about time healing and absence making the heart grow fonder are true. No one
could fill that space inside me that belongs to

you. I hope more than you do that one day you'll slip back in.

Instead I said, "The worst is over, Dad. And I can't wait to see what half of you is going to look like."

"Probably like Tom Selleck, I should think," he said with a straight face.

Against my will I smiled. He noticed and seemed pleased. We stood to make our way back to the parking lot.